MONSIEUR

JEAN LORRAIN, born Paul Alexandre Martin Duval, was a novelist, critic, and dramatist, and one of the most conspicuously Decadent figures of *fin-de-siècle* France. He was born in Fécamp, France, on August 9, 1855, to a family of shipowners. In 1876, he began studying law, which he abandoned in 1878 to haunt the newsrooms and cafés of Paris, as well as *Le Chat Noir* cabaret. He later frequented Charles Buet's salon, where he met Joris-Karl Huysmans, Léon Bloy, and Jules Barbey d'Aurevilly (who is said to have inspired the character Monsieur de Bougrelon). Lorrain's columns appeared regularly in *L'Écho de Paris, L'Événement,* and *Le Courrier français,* securing Lorrain a reputation as the era's most scathing critic. He had run-ins with many of the 1890s' most influential figures and dueled with Marcel Proust after Lorrain critiqued the young author's *Les Plaisirs et les Jours.* In 1895, Lorrain's friend Edmond de Goncourt wondered, "What's Lorrain's dominant trait? Is it spite or a complete lack of tact?" In 1891, Lorrain's first collection of short stories, *Sonyeuse,* was published. He followed up on this success with additional collections of stories and poetry that, in translator Stephen Romer's words, transformed Lorrain's experiences "into some of the most memorable disturbing tales of the age." Masks and disguises are recurring themes in these stories, as is Parisian low life, satanism, ether, homosexuality, and the aristocracy. In 1897, critics hailed his novel *Monsieur de Bougrelon;* however, his health was deteriorating, and in 1900, Lorrain left Paris to live in Nice. His stay at the Riviera began an intense period of creativity. In 1901, he wrote his best-known work, *Monsieur de Phocas,* which he followed a year later with his fantastical aristocrat saga, *Le Vice errant.* His health continued to decline due to syphilis and his abuse of drugs. He died on June 30, 1906, of peritonitis, at the age of fifty-one. He was buried in his hometown of Fécamp. It was rumored that when Lorrain's grave was opened in 1986, the body of "Sodom's ambassador to Paris," as biographer Philippe Jullian called him, still smelled of ether.

Eva Richter translated *My Suicide* by Swiss author Henri Roorda, published by Spurl Editions. Her writing has been featured in Columbia University's *Catch & Release,* and as an editor for the translation journal *Asymptote,* she edited Marcel Schwob's *Mimes* (1901) in English translation.

JEAN LORRAIN

MONSIEUR DE BOUGRELON

TRANSLATED BY EVA RICHTER

SPURL EDITIONS

Cover photo: A male memento mori figure used
for spiritual contemplation – Wellcome Library, London

Originally published in French by Librairie Borel in 1897

Translation and afterword copyright ©2016 Eva Richter

Published by Spurl Editions

ISBN: 978-1-943679-03-4

Spurl Editions
www.spurleditions.com
spurlcontact@gmail.com

CONTENTS

MONSIEUR DE BOUGRELON

To you, my dear Pozzi, who knew him and loved him, allow me to dedicate this Monsieur de Bougrelon.

J. L.
October 1902

CHAPTER ONE

CAFÉ MANCHESTER

Amsterdam, it is always water and houses painted black and
white, all windows, with sculpted gables and lace curtains; the
black, the white splinter in the water. And so it is always water,
dead water, iridescent water and gray water, alleys of water that
do not end, canals guarded by dwellings like enormous dom-
inos; it could be gloomy, and yet it is not sad, but eventually it
is a bit monotonous, especially when the water freezes and the
gelid pewter of the canals no longer reflects the small, pretty
dollhouses, upside down with front steps high in the air.

There was a strong wind on the Amstel that day, a wind to
sweep away the sweepers themselves. At the Dam, there was
the spectacle (which we had already seen too many times)
of the tram station and the crowds around it; of fur caps
pulled down over violet ears, cabmen and drivers blossoming
with rosacea, necks disappearing behind mufflers, and those
strange little old men who, with eternal drops of frost on the
ends of their red noses, hawk omnibus connections at the

highest prices. But everyone needs to live, and the surprise of hearing *dangüe* for *merci,* and the surprise of gathering freezing snot from the back of their gloved hands is one of the pleasures of tourism in Amsterdam.

Oh, these people of the North! The Dutch man, by the way, is rather ugly, and the Dutch woman resembles him. Those old women in black velvet hats perched upon caps of lace, embellished at the temple with hemstitched medallions of gold, apparently work better in the old master paintings than they do in the streets. And the Zeedijk (the Rietdijk of Amsterdam) does not come to life until nighttime. As for the Nes – where good, shapely, strapping men, very blond and very pink, innocently approach you from dive bar entrances, their plump bodies bulging out of their long hotel porters' cloaks and their faces radiant – it had lost its mystery for us: we had already visited it too many times as well. This is surely human ingratitude, because the Nes had so delighted us the first night!

We used to love those heavy doors that opened abruptly to reveal, behind a row of tables, a heap of flesh and spangles, raised like a dessert on a faraway, luminous platform. "*Dames françaises!* Come in, Messieurs, we speak French," and this from the decent, chubby-cheeked giants, who bowed and smiled with full lips, but they were good, honest smiles, unknown in Paris; they did not release for a minute the doorkeeper's ropes they held in their hands. Indeed, at every entrance on Nesstraat there was the same sudden appearance of nudity and dazzling fabrics, the same patriotic offer, *dames françaises,* and the same salute.

Oh, only French women on every Nes, from the Belgian fogs to the distant parts of Holland, they are in every region!

Oh! How we are happy to be French
When we travel to foreign lands.[†]

Amsterdam's red-light districts are relaxing and refresh the soul; there is a sense of geniality there that is unknown in the Latin countries, and these devilish exhibitors, these solid doorkeepers to hell, defuse malice with their good shiny faces and their good thick hands in fur gloves, looking like thoroughly honest major-domos under their gold-tasseled caps. But apparently we had seen too much of them.

Nes, Zeedijk, the Dam, and even the museum did not speak to us anymore; there are days like that in life. We wandered through the city like flotsam, along the frozen canals, hurrying around street corners, for the great wind, as I have already said, blew forcefully that day on the Amstel.

It was bone-chilling outside, savagely cold, and the many *Schiedammers*[‡] we had knocked back in every cellar on Kalverstraat had hardly perked us up – there are days like that in life too – and so we meandered under January's north wind, pitiable and glum, when an odd sign captivated us:

[†] *"Ah! qu'on est fier d'être Français / Quand on voyage à l'étranger."* These lines are likely derived from the song "La Colonne" (1818) by Émile Debraux. Its lyrics are: *"Ah! qu'on est fier d'être Français / Quand on regarde la Colonne."*

[‡] A juniper-flavored liquor similar to gin, produced in Schiedam, in the Netherlands. It is also called "jenever" or "genever."

Café Manchester.

It was in one of those uniform black-and-white Amsterdam streets: a small old two-story dwelling, very low beneath an enormous roof that crowned it from its gable nearly to the first floor. The lodging seemed packed in on itself, as though squeezed underground, and we had to descend five steps to find the front door and the only window, hung with wide net curtains of taut guipure, which opened just above the ground; on the other levels there were small irregular dormer windows with closed shutters. *Café Manchester!* It had the look of a lantern. It even had a pulley at the top of its roof to raise supplies and furniture. What did they sell in this café? In this Café Manchester, where apparently they spoke French as well as English.

The cold was intense, the house dubious; we went inside.

"Take your seats, Messieurs, sit! The women are coming. Déborah, hey! Gudule, French gentlemen are here."

An old venerable woman spoke (a wide black velvet bonnet rested upon her lace cap), an old woman in a shawl, in bracelets and cameos, and Déborah entered the little low room with minuet steps, a great toothy smile, and, with knees bent, three curtseys. The girls are far less polite in France – and what style! What modesty, and what distinction! . . . We took our seats. Oh, what a cozy interior! The table was polished and shiny, the furniture waxed until it reflected, and the washed walls gleamed like moiré silk, with reflections cast throughout and a good earthenware stove in the back . . . There was even a rack made of island wood, a pipe rack, with pipes that Jan Peters and Cornelis surely once smoked at night; it was charming, but the girls were less so.

Low . . . waisted and short-legged, as blond as a towline, with an absentminded profile and a flushed complexion, Déborah was overfamiliar, even eager.

With a playful temper, she could have pleased at the age of eighteen, but Café Manchester had evidently fattened her and given her wrinkles, and the poor good girl, as red as roast beef and as curly-haired as a sheep, deplorably insisted on climbing onto our knees and dipping into our glasses.

Her cheeks, scrubbed with sand like copper pitchers, were blindingly radiant.

Déborah was nice and rinsed thoroughly, much like the interior of a Dutch house, but her hair was thinning, the blue of her eyes was bland, and her soft skin exuded a heady musky scent. As it happened, though, she had an affectionate, even caressing, nature, with hands that were easily led astray, and she was touchingly obstinate in repeating to you, "Be gentle, Monsieur, don't fight it!"

Gudule tempted even less. Called out by the house *patronne* the moment she tried to soap up the floor of one of the upper rooms, this pretty servant girl (a real workhorse) rushed down the stairs in the makeshift outfit of a proper worker – a linen shift thrown over an underskirt, her feet naked in clogs.

"To serve you, Monsieur!" She dove into a brusque curtsy. "Beer is on you, right?"

And Gudule made herself at home.

If Déborah stank of musk, Gudule had a strong smell of hot water and potash, but her breasts were firm and the skin of her arms was as granular and prickly as a turkey's; her washerwoman's arms could have pleased only cart drivers. Beneath her sleeves, boldly rolled up, she was a mean peasant woman, interested neither in her pitcher of beer nor in men's kisses, a real Teniers, with a square figure and hard limbs; her face, though, was rather ugly, and her smile had a few holes – the humidity of the Netherlands is so catastrophic to delicate dentition!

Déborah had lighted a lamp. The woman in the black hat, seated at a distance, had put on a pair of enormous spectacles and was keeping herself busy, her nose in her knitting, maneuvering long thin needles. From time to time she ventured a quick, discreet look at us, a debonair smile, a mute "go on, my children, don't be ashamed" that reassured and soothed, like a blanket of cotton creating tranquility and security. We had already bought Déborah five *Schiedammers* and Gudule four bottles of beer. Oh, the peaceful and homely Dutch interior!

It was at that moment that He appeared.

He, Him, the epic silhouette of this misty country, of this city of dreams, the prestigious hero of this tale.

He flung the door open with a single motion, installed himself in the entrance, and waited.

What an entrance! The man who arrives this way surely must have a gift.

Swaggering, with his waist cinched in a big piped redingote,[†] his shoulders broad and his chest thin, and an enormous top hat tilted to one side, not to mention the terrifying cudgel he held in his hand, he was a familiar character, and particularly unforgettable. He had the demeanor of a prison guard, of an old leading man, of a *demi-solde*;[‡] he was at once Javert, Napoleon's retreat from Russia, and Frédérick Lemaître! His redingote was green, and what a threadbare green! His pants, attached by boot straps, twisted screw-like into his heeled boots, which were thin and polished, though ripped open at the toe; his muffler of red wool, so very long around his neck, was a darned and patched-together rag full of holes; but inasmuch as this tatterdemalion was a great nobleman – with his face of an old Capitano,[§] made up and powdered white, his bloodshot eyes blackened with charcoal, and his mouth toothless beneath the double-comma of his waxed mustache – this puppet personified a race, his mask a soul.

The two girls had gotten up. Still planted firmly in the door frame, where his silhouette grew and grew, the man had crossed his arms, and, holding his cudgel against his chest, he now bent backward and smiled.

"Oh, my little kittens!" grumbled the cavernous voice.

[†] The redingote originated as a variation of the English "riding coat." It evolved into a greatcoat, similar to a frock coat, that was long and pinched at the waist. *Demi-soldes* were known to wear civilian redingotes (frequently green) to hide their threadbare uniforms.

[‡] An officer who served in the Napoleonic armies, forced into semi-retired, reserve status during the Bourbon Restoration.

[§] A reference to *Il Capitano*, a stock character of the Italian *commedia dell'arte*. He was the prototype of a pretentious, yet cowardly, military man.

"Are you not excited for my delicacies today? I have sugared almonds for you anyway. I know you are usually big eaters."

And, with a gesture of a bygone court, he spread a few small grains of snuff on the back of his hand, then returned his squalid box of white wood to his waistcoat pocket. With a snort of his large nostrils, he inhaled the dose in a single pull.

"Real Spanish tobacco, which a friend, the Marquis de Las Marimas Tolosas, sends me every year from Havana, and which today you will go without, Mesdemoiselles, because I find you ungrateful. We forget our old friend. Your passing lovers are having fun at your expense, my doves! And if these men are not French . . . Oh, if you are not French, Messieurs, I am warning you, there will be an uproar. Yes, Messieurs, an uproar to be settled tomorrow, in the countryside. But I am only too happy to greet my compatriots here. These little maniacs would have hardly fêted you so much if you had been Dutch. They are romantics in love with Paris. Myself, I am from the Île-de-France, more Parisian than Madame de Staël, who was born on Rue du Bac; I am from the suburbs, the suburbs, that ring of scum and Lutetia's flowers, and from a truly charming area, Bas-Meudon, Messieurs. The ferry used to stop at the bottom of my father's château terrace three times a day. Alas, *la bande noire* destroyed that."

And, pausing, he discovered that his head was bald, but bald only for a moment, because almost immediately the wig that had been carried away in the lining of his hat fell back upon his skull; he then very nobly announced, "My name is Monsieur de Bougrelon, Messieurs! Gin, Déborah, and my own gin for me."

When the girl had placed before the old puppet a Delft bottle that was as big and potbellied as a goat udder in its wicker corbelling, he went on, "I drink nothing but 1850 – these drugs need forty years in a bottle. Brought from the Indies, northern alcohols are sometimes marvelous, but to tell you the truth, this one here never sailed. It is quite flavorful anyway. Will you have some, Messieurs?"

He spoke with his head raised, in the haughty, declamatory tone of a theater patriarch, his stomach bulging like a ship's bow, his shoulders exaggeratedly thrown back. Déborah had filled our glasses, and he grabbed her as she passed and sat her on his knees; what an extravagant and almost tragic duo, with that slattern straddling the bony thigh of that ancestor with the head of a specter, a swaggering, dirty old specter, for he had slid one hand beneath the girl's skirts, while the other, a withered mummy's hand, obviously better-looking in former times (now macabre under the heavy gilt copper rings he wore on every finger), smoothed his stiff dyed mustache; and it was almost a scene from Holbein in the glimmering half-light of the dive, as the heavy pink girl, too blond and too fleshy, rubbed and caressed the painted cadaver, who was corseted, made up, and necktied beneath his red muffler, like a rogue of the Régence, a cascade of gold lace . . . .[†]
Prostitution Caressing Death. But Monsieur de Bougrelon did not relent.

"You arrived in Amsterdam recently, Messieurs? May I ask

[†] The ellipses appear in the French edition.

when? You have already explored the city, visited the museum, the churches, and the girls. But by goodness, Amsterdam is a mysterious city. Its houses seem transparent, open to any riffraff; it is all windows here, or so the visitor believes; and we self-satisfied people (we all are in France), after three strolls in the city, believe we have mastered the Dutch women and Holland itself, Rotterdam and The Hague, the Zuiderzee even, why, the whole North Sea! A mistake, Messieurs! Holland is a tease: she offers everything and gives nothing. The water of her canals is too deep; it reflects the boats above, which never sink, though if they were to sink, we would not see them again. Amsterdam, Rotterdam, and all the Dams of the world are built on chasms, on stilts – consider that!

"I want to steer you over these stilts, Messieurs. Your insouciant ignorance charms me and moves me to pity. I am not smug about this. Honestly, it is delicious: Amsterdam's houses appeared to be made of glass to you, though they are made of horn, Messieurs! Adultery flourishes here like tulips, but it rejects any foreign fertilizer. The city is all windows, you say, but there are no doors! Or very few. They are dollhouses here, but much more dangerous, because the doll is a woman, a woman who is gussied up, made up, utterly futile and lying, for she is empty and has no soul, and it is this void that attracts us, us men; this chasm, it is the eternal chasm of the Dam cities on stilts."

Suddenly he interrupted his lecture to sniff Déborah's camisole.

"Your skin is very fine, my girl, but your musk is poisoning me. Where did you get that perfume? The barber who sold it to you must be a roast cook. You are prepared in goose grease! Tomorrow I will send you a bottle of bergamot and a jar of almond paste steeped in amaryllis sap."

Rising abruptly, with a flick of his finger Monsieur de Bougrelon brushed off the snuff grains that remained on his gold lace, casually took up his cane, and left the bill for us to settle.

"Amsterdam awaits us. Allow me to do the honors."

Since the two girls, like beggars, were following us to the door, he added, "A little modesty, Mesdemoiselles! Do you take us for sailors? Do you not see that these men are gentlemen? We will return."

Flemish gibberish, insults surely, answered this promise; they booed our departure. Then an extraordinary thing happened. Gudule, who I had thought was so gentle, furious at seeing Monsieur de Bougrelon leading her clients away, grabbed him by his waist – his slender, contoured waist – and lifted him off the earth in her solid arms, spinning him like so much straw in an aerial pirouette before placing him back on the ground to a huge rash of insults and laughter at the old man's feebleness.

"She is a bit familiar," Monsieur de Bougrelon merely said. "One suffocates in this hovel."

CHAPTER TWO

MONSIEUR DE MORTIMER

We were walking together for some time when the road opened onto a view of a canal.

"A beautiful sight, geometric and calm," our strange companion interrupted. "One of the only ones perfectly suited for restless souls. I have been living in Holland for nearly thirty years, Messieurs. The adventure that brought me here is a bit melancholy, and, as you've already guessed, it was an adventure of love. Yes, it has been some thirty years now since I left France. We first settled down in The Hague, Monsieur de Mortimer and I, for I exiled myself for a man. Although naturally there was a woman involved too. In 1840, we still had such heroic friendships. When Mortimer was forced to leave Avranches after his duel with Lord Finghal, I followed him. Should I have let him move away alone, to be far from his family, his friends, his home – a friend of more than twenty years, a man whom all of my mistresses were crazy about, and who, in our more than two hundred matches, always disarmed me in the third round but never gloried in his victory?

"In our more than twenty years together, we kept the same women and the same horses, and when, in that unfortunate duel with Lord Finghal, Monsieur de Mortimer's loyalty was doubted . . . I did not hesitate . . .

"Mortimer! The great *enfant terrible* ignited terrible grudges in our small town of Avranches; he was strangely beautiful, and that is the only thing that men cannot forgive another man for. He was proud too, and his pride was so charming that it enraged the many prigs of the province. Realize, too, Messieurs, that this beloved man never breathed a word of his good fortune to others, just so that he would not have enemies!

"So we emigrated together. Paris, where the fat Duke of Orléans had reigned, was too small for us, and so it was The Hague that sheltered us first. Yes, The Hague had this honor, The Hague and its royal museum, where so many of the beautiful portraits appeared to us as our very own likenesses, for I was handsome then in my own way too. We turned quite a few heads in The Hague; the aristocratic and tranquil city was at our feet, and in the evenings, at the court balls, the sigh of *'another unfortunate is coming for me,'* with which Mortimer greeted every woman's entrance, was not simply the brash hyperbole that one might have at first believed. Who could have resisted his prestigious elegance, his profile of a young god, but a god of Versailles, majestic as a Bourbon, insolent as a Lauzun, a royal god, a true gentleman god.

"He brought the refined bearing and studied disposition of our royalist Normandy, which must have subjugated the barbaric people of Zeeland! Oh! If you had seen him strolling through the park, in two-four time, on those foggy winter days, or even greeting the beautiful women arranged in a quincunx around the fish pond on those frosty mornings after Mass at the château! There were sable stoles worth fifty *louis* a skin, Messieurs; cloaks of bishop's violet wool lined with blue fox[†] pelts; real sappers' caps and enormous muffs of spaniel fur, as blond as a woman's hair, from which Monsieur de Mortimer would pull out a single hand gloved in black sealskin to greet the royal children. These were extraordinary gloves, Messieurs, with every finger festooned at the tip with agate, a tiger's paw, or a devil's hand: an invention all his own, an utterly delicious eccentricity, and one that reflected him! Yes, it was he who first wore a black velvet hat with a large buckle of Cape diamonds on a high moiré ribbon; and when he went out at night, he would powder his mustache, which was blond and very handsome, with an odd mélange of blue powder and gold. From a distance, one would have sworn it was a scarab, an Egyptian scarab placed upon a red rose, because, until the last day, he had the most vermilion lips, as though he had painted them with the blood of hearts.

"How to resist fantasies like these?

"And this hero was forced to exile himself because of some small aristocrat in the court of Caen. Mortimer, after all, was Norman like me. The two of us came from this race of giants, a strong blond race, which dares to conquer and dares to love, a race of imperishable adventurers whose blue blood

[†] Reference to the arctic fox.

still flourishes in the meadows of London, an immortal race whose uncurbable spirit of adventure conquered England, the Indies, and all its colonies.

"Thus it was over some small aristocrat, a spiteful Noble of the Robe of negligible beauty, that Mortimer fought with Lord Finghal, colonel in the Highlanders' third regiment, on leave in our old city of Caen; in winter, our lush and mild-weathered Normandy attracted many of these long-legged wading birds from across the Channel. Madame de Bresveville was watched closely by Lord Finghal, and so, as a mere bagatelle, my friend began courting this ninny and provoked her impertinent ogler until finally, from twenty paces away on a park lane, he blew off the Englishman's head, though in such a singular fashion that it put the police on our heels. The most unexpected fate, truly a prestigious stroke of luck, had Lord Finghal killed by his own bullet . . . Monsieur de Mortimer had a skull that was so hard, a skull of granite, Messieurs, that the cursed Englishman's bullet ricocheted off his forehead and swiftly killed our good Highlander. He fell in a heap at the end of the lane, his head smashed to bits, and even Mortimer could not get over it. 'I repel bullets,' he merely said as he handed me his weapon.

"That night we had to hurry away from the city. They accused us of murder! They even claimed that I, Mortimer's witness, had aimed for and killed my friend's adversary! They accused us of nothing else! They truly did not know us at all! A despicable plot, Messieurs, and indeed worthy of a city where country-bumpkin lawyers, whose ancestors served meals, sat on the bench! We cleared out at nightfall, persuaded but not convinced by the Marquise de Brindecourt, who lent us her carriage. We could not resist the tears of this noble white-haired woman. Mortimer cherished her like his own mother, whom he never knew; the dowager had raised him in her lap, for this big-hearted woman could not bear to see the august kneecaps on which Mortimer played as a child crawling along the paving stones . . . We left, Monsieur, and rain fell on that gloomiest of nights. That sad night! It seemed that Normandy's entire sky was crying. We never returned to that place, and it is thus that the last descendant of a race of champions, which should have never died out, spoiled his most beautiful future, and all for a little towheaded woman whom you would have never glanced at in Paris. *C'est la vie.* A bump in the road can make even a giant stumble.

"But I must leave you now, Messieurs. I have a rendezvous and could have hardly predicted this agreeable meeting. A noblewoman who thinks very fondly of me awaits; besides, you surely feel at home on Kalverstraat. I am at your service tomorrow, if you do not find me a nuisance. Your hotel? I can be there at nine o'clock, in full regalia, and I am only too happy to show you a few spots in Amsterdam worthy of your curiosity."

A great tip of his hat, a sudden straightening of his long torso: he had vanished.

CHAPTER THREE

THE RUBY ROSARY

"The museum! I will take you to the museum."

On the stroke of nine, as he had said the night before, Monsieur de Bougrelon was at our hotel. His leg a bit stiff, but with a nonetheless majestic gait, he strode across the lobby, his chest more impertinently straightened than usual, scandalizing the proper Dutch people who were gorging themselves at tables laden with mortadella slices, dry sausages, and immense bowlfuls of café au lait.

We had been warned by the hotel porter, who had gone up to our rooms to let us know that a traveling entertainer was asking for us downstairs, and we had immediately guessed what was afoot.

A traveling entertainer! The old Norman gentleman, the son of former pirates, conquerors of the three islands! Everywhere, abroad and in France, flunkeys have the same crass irreverence for all who are heroic in misery, who remain grandiloquent in rags.

We rushed down to avoid the last representative of an illustrious race being snubbed.

We were right on time: the hotel's entire staff, not to mention travelers who had descended from the *Adrian,* guests, valets, and sommeliers, had formed a circle around Monsieur de Mortimer's distinguished friend; and indeed, this morning Monsieur de Bougrelon had outdone himself. To honor us, the old dandy had put on such a remarkable fur hat and houppelande[†] of Carmelite-brown cloth that he took our breath away. With frogging of olive silk, and with more decorative trim than a Hungarian hussar's jacket, the coat was cinched at the waist and flapped around his knees, an unexpected outfit even in Amsterdam, where passersby still dressed like Admiral de Ruyter. In fact, it was everything one could want except a simple coat: Argan the Hypochondriac's robe, a Caucasus leader's caftan, a Warsaw Jew's pelisse, something unnameable, something extravagant, and yet still reminiscent of the retreat from Russia, an epic rag that would have made a theater star's fortune on a boulevard stage. An old sealskin cap, as large as a sombrero, crowned that ancient spectral head; Russian leather boots, with silver spurs with enormous spinning wheels, completed the outfit. Finally, in his two hands the old puppet held a phenomenal muff (once black, now russet) close to his chest: the muff had been curled, straightened, skinned; apparently an old poodle's hide! The monster smiled and in a peremptory tone said, "I went to great lengths. What do you think of me?"

[†] A loose, long outer garment, open in the front, with wide sleeves, belted, and sometimes padded or lined with fur.

Prancing in place, he went on, "Could your tailors in Paris cut a houppelande like this out of their Elbeuf cloth? Feel the texture of this material – see how it hugs my waist without constricting my hips! What freedom in the shoulders! I am at home. And this cap! It is of virgin seal, Messieurs. When I wore it for the first time, I was at the lake in Groningen, ice skating in the park. The Duchess Wilhelmine (an exquisite woman, there are no more like her) gave us a night of celebration there. With costumes, sleds, torches, and masks, it was one of the last enchanted spectacles of the century. The Duchess dressed up as a Mongolian princess, and I dressed as a lord from Greenland. We did not leave each other all night, and for an entire week after, the *Gazette de La Haye* talked about that Mongolian princess and that duke from Greenland. Monsieur de Mortimer donned the fabulous garb of a Samarkand sultan. My goodness! We knew how to spend money, we emigrants. I had this cap made for the ball: I call it a ball, yet we skated, and above all, we traded, traded amorous words, elegant, musky, and frivolous words, passionate, futile, and somber words, because one died sometimes, yes, died, to exchange a glance, to clutch a hand in the shadows, who knows, to get a surprise kiss! Yes, we were like that. So I had this cap made for that exquisite night and for the woman who was even more exquisite. A few gold tassels and pearl frills brightened my cap then, though the pearls later fell off. Now they are in a nostalgic frame around an ivory portrait miniature that you will see at my home when you do me the honor of coming through my door, Messieurs. I removed the gold tassels myself, as I did those on my boots. A person must know how to sacrifice to our epoch's prejudices; sometimes we must just resign ourselves to the preconceived ideas of our dearest friends, *n'est-ce pas?*"

With a very thin smile, he said, "Understand, Messieurs, that if I still received my previous one hundred thousand *livres* of income, my elegance would be more discreet, but poverty owes it to itself to be ostentatious. Only millionaires have the right to soot-colored clothes."

His great ankylotic body did a nimble pirouette.

"The museum! Messieurs, I will take you to the museum."

As we were walking down the street, he said in a melancholy tone, "I always cause a ruckus here. As backward as this country is, it has moved on, but me, I stayed in place. I am an idea in an era that has no more of them. Though you are new in Amsterdam, you look like one of their own to these people, while I, who have lived with them for forty years, I . . . But the strange is a stranger everywhere. Loyalty is quite eccentric, what can I say? It is too bad that this eccentricity means exile, Messieurs. Who is loyal in these times? The exile is always alone. Anyway, I am proud of my solitude. I am being pilloried here, and yet I dominate the crowd. What could matter to me now, after I experienced a sublime friendship and lived in the company of ideal women – the last women, you understand, who belonged to a society that is gone forever – what could matter to me? I will tell you. The little fearful cries of the bourgeois in their windows? The street urchins turning around to get a second look at me? The passersby's jeers at the religion of the past? They tease me, and that puts me at ease, yes, at ease, and even better: I just don't give a damn about these nobodies!"

As we were acquiescing with a smile to the touching sadness of his bragging, he said, "Do you like museums, Messieurs? Monsieur de Mortimer and I spent the best hours of our exile in them. Oh, the women's portraits! How the painted gazes of certain portraits cast spells on us! I don't know if you feel as I do, Messieurs? There is magic in some faces done by the old masters. You wouldn't know it by looking at me now, but when I lived in Florence (for I once lived in Italy), I spent two hours at the Uffizi every morning. I had three mistresses there, all three of them dead, who could have made my living mistresses jealous, and with good reason; in fact, time has turned all the living women I knew, with one exception, to ashes and tears, while those three portraits . . . One was a Leonardo, as you have guessed. A man like me always loves da Vinci. The other was a Luini, and it showed a courtesan with red hair, but red as only the Italians knew how to paint it, with pearls and rubies plaited into her golden braids. I say a courtesan, Herodias surely, for she carried – and with what a gesture! – a bloody head on a gilded silver dish, and as hideous as this head was, with its serous pallor and contorted eyes, I wanted this head to be my own; beheading for beheading, I would have consented to it, if only to be so triumphantly carried by this triumphant woman. This Herodias had arched eyebrows and an arched mouth, with brows so black and a mouth so royally made up that I was triply lovestruck. Oh! Those three stretched arches! Cupid was hiding behind each one of them, and it was a triple trigger, a triple attack, to the head first, then right to the heart, and finally . . . you know where. A terrible woman, terrible and exquisite, but I had reason to love her. Indecently and dangerously, she resembled a certain adorable, savage Spanish woman. I said Spanish woman and I see you smile. I should have known her in Paris, for this Spanish woman was of a great race, Messieurs; she was born Della Morozina Campéador Cantès, and she was a heroic woman.

"Married at thirteen years old to a Mexican general who was killed during the insurrection, she witnessed the capture of Puebla; what's more, she defended it! She had a portrait of her husband tattooed on her left breast, and when she stripped for the ball, this glimpsed tattoo looked like a lace pattern, a scrap of mantilla upon her white skin; it was divine, an exquisite refinement of coquetry, an epic tattoo that made her more beautiful. We would have liked to erase the image of her husband from her bosom with the force of our kisses, but it was indelible, and the Marquise Della Morozina Campéador Cantès was unattainable. At the capture of Puebla, she had suffered the horrors of rape, foul rape, Messieurs. Twenty insurgent leaders had argued with pistol shots over the savage delight of possessing her first, firing two hundred bullets until five maniacs perished. This unfortunate woman bore the brunt of the fifteen left, who were boiling with lust and carnage, while leaning upon the five still-warm cadavers, and she did not die, Messieurs! Though she did take a vow of chastity.

"A woman who is truly a woman, who knew the horrible

pleasure of fifteen rapes and is protected by memory: the Marquise was one of these. She was a soul walled away in terror, a body frozen in outrage.

"And yet, what coquetry! She brought the most beautiful gems from Mexico, but from her unbelievable jewel box she wore nothing but rubies – bloody stones on a woman once bloodied – which she wore like a monk wears a hair shirt, and in this way the passionate savagery of her soul broke out. She wore these rubies without a setting: fifteen testimonial rubies (in memory of her fifteen violators), encrusted in her skin.

"They were fifteen drops of blood that formed translucent beads upon her bare flesh; fifteen glittering gems on her shoulders, which were pierced with fifteen wounds; fifteen scars that opened again each time she went to a ball, Messieurs, for if she was too much of a flirt to renounce the world, she still tortured her body in expiation, and her jewels became her tormentor. Admit it, one must be terribly smug to dare speak of love to a woman who wears around her neck the bloody memory of fifteen rapes, with a portrait of her husband on her left breast. And what a portrait! Tattooed, Messieurs, as I have said.

"Yet one night someone had such terrible smugness, such inconceivable and juvenile audacity, Messieurs, and this person was not Monsieur de Mortimer, and this person was not Monsieur de Lafretté-Junance, the handsomest of the king's guards, it was . . . But here we are at the museum! We have arrived."

And with the awkwardness of a child, he said, "I told you,

Messieurs, that I wildly adored and loved Luini's *Herodias* for the way it resembled her. So I compromised the Marquise . . . which would have been cowardly if this exquisite woman had had the slightest weakness for me.

"The Marquise Della Morozina Campéador Cantès," and here Monsieur de Bougrelon took off his hat, "the Marquise Della Morozina Campéador Cantès died, twenty years ago, secluded in Avranches, in a small house that still belonged to me until two years ago. I have sold it since then, and that is one of the great sorrows of my life.

"Ruined by bankers, the Marquise Della Morozina Campéador Cantès was happy to accept the modest pension that I could give her for eight years of her life; she was happy to accept it because, having never been my mistress, she could." Monsieur de Bougrelon spoke with his hat in his hand all the while. "A Marquise Della Morozina cannot be kept and looked after like a girl, but a gallant man can help a friend. That is how we once were in Avranches.

"Mércèdes, for she was called Mércèdes, perhaps thought of me in her final hour. Now the rosary on which I say my Paternoster (you will see it at my home above her miniature) has three big rubies for each of the Lord's Prayers."

CHAPTER FOUR

NOSTALGIC DOLLS

Long spells cast by the archaic eyes
Of the Louvre's painted women,
In their sides, wounds open and cry,
And give Her a pale face and haggard guise.

"I have had this same side wound my entire life, Messieurs, because for my entire life, I have been an unhappy and mad lover of old portraits. These verses, scribbled in my youth (for I once was a poet too, just like the others), still describe the wild nostalgia of my soul, my nostalgic and proud soul, which made me, from age eighteen to twenty-five, the ecstatic devotee of the museums of Dresden and Italy. Monsieur de Mortimer had it also, this soul. Our friendship was a Eucharist: we communed over the same admirations, and we loved each other through our shared hatreds. You would find us kneeling at the altar of the masters then, although we would rise in the chapel of the beauties: inclined before Art, upright before Beauty. Oh! The smiles of da Vinci, Messieurs – a poem of perverse, royal ferocity, of leeches' kisses that engulfed our souls. The *Mona Lisa* sucked away everything I had.

"And Botticelli's women, the grace of their fleeting, willowy nudity, the excitement of their slender bodies, the *Primavera* especially! As I stand before you, Messieurs, I confess that for two years I was in love with that ghoul-faced nymph, for it is a ghoul, and maybe worse! The ambiguity of its sex made both of us anxious, feverish, exasperated. Naturally Monsieur de Mortimer and I always had the same mistresses, whether alive or dead, though we preferred the dead for the pointlessness of our passion, steeped like a sword in the lava and sulfur of despair ... A true suffering for Art, that is what our youth was like, our youth ...

Beset by futile longing for futile nostalgia!

"As I wrote somewhere, in the last tercet of a sonnet that I dedicated to Monsieur de Mortimer, I believe (in fact, yes, I remember now, and what a sonnet!), I compared him – and I even moved myself to pity – to someone bewitched by Gothic magic, because this love of ghosts (and aren't all portraits ghosts?) stinks, admit it, of potions and charms and, as I told him in this sonnet, of spellbooks and looking glasses (in which I was reflected too), and in these three verses, I attested to our enchantment:

From then on, obsessed by the captivating charms
Of the Dead, insensible to the charms of the Living,

Your heart searched for beauty only in the past,
    Edgard?

"His name was Edgard, like the Master of Ravenswood, and this Edgard was not missing his Lucy, although his Lucy was *nevermore,* and not from *Lammermoor.* Nevermore: in life as in dreams, Messieurs, his motto and our motto was this knell of pride. Nevermore.

"But, truthfully, how can you become enamored – what am I saying, how can you fall head over heels in love with a museum portrait in this coarse, greasy Holland? They are Beguines, Messieurs, with sparse hair and missing eyebrows, their faces pink and faded. Have you by chance tasted their salmon-colored skin? Fishwives, they are fishwives, worse, chilblains upon gadrooned ruffs . . .

"What about the pinks and pearly whites of the Flemish School, you will perhaps object? You are trying to hoodwink me: they are the pinks and pearly whites of shrimp. The Flemish School is a fishmonger's stall, when it isn't fresh cuts of meat hanging on hooks in Rubens' butcher shops . . . Talk to me of Velázquez, rather! Though his *Infantas* have heads of wax and hair of silk floss, a person could fall in love with those dolls. There are reflections of the auto-da-fé in the moiré and the satins of their robes; and the roses they disdainfully hold at their fingertips, those roses are red with all the blood of the Jews whose throats were cut at cathedral entrances. Oh, and how deliciously tainted they are with it all! . . . Velázquez is indeed the painter of the old aristocracies! Here he is, the lavish historian of the end of a race of kings.

> *Before a pale infanta with delicate hands*
> *Sketched within a billowy cascade of lampas and moiré,*
> *Relive, oh King of Spain, deep inside your sinister*
> *Palaces, your tragic glories and commands.*

"That, Messieurs, is not a Bougrelon, but a Mortimer. Like me, he had an unbridled passion for the Spanish School! And Goya, Messieurs, fantasy in reality! And Coello! And Antonio Moro! And perhaps the most marvelous of all, the sublime in the horrible, El Greco! Infernal and celestial at once, for what is hell but heaven reversed?[†] The others had suns, pearls, babies' skin, and roses on their palettes; but El Greco, he dipped his brush in the bloody wounds of the anatomical subjects he drew with his fierce charcoal, and he seized his charcoal from the pyre of the Holy Inquisition. With what dark intensity he burned his heretics in his painting at El Escorial! He was a highly devoted Catholic, and these Dutch stink of the Reformation.

"Did you visit Sint-Baafskathedraal in Haarlem? It is a sepulcher. It is paved with tombstones . . . You walk on the dead there, and God is absent, just as in the basilica of Basel. Me, I hate, and with such a sweet hatred, these Protestant moths. Luther is a shadow upon the century. Catholicism was red; Protestantism is worse, because it has no color. It is neu-

[†] ". . . *car l'enfer, c'est le ciel en creux.*" This is a direct reference to the French author Jules Barbey d'Aurevilly, who famously wrote, "*L'enfer, c'est le ciel en creux.*"

tral and marches through history dressed in a gray drugget, like an old peasant. It did away with stained-glass windows (that says it all) and brought back wimples up to the chin. It was the abolition of breasts and blessed saints, of everything that opens your eyes and makes them glow . . . Looking up at the blazing stained glass of queens in bejeweled robes and naked archangels, you glimpsed a bit of the heavens living in the vaulting. Seeing the women's bare necks jutting out of their bodices was a bit of love, a bit of paradise, in the gray monotony of the days.

"Protestantism was the death of joy, Messieurs, and it was also the death of luxury and lust. You will refute me with Rubens and Van Dyck – a slap in the face! I will answer that Rubens was an ambassador, he knew the Venice School and painted for a Luxembourg queen who was the most Italian, what am I saying, the most Florentine of our queens; I called her Marie de Médicis. As for Van Dyck, he lived in the English court, and in the most sumptuous and elegant court, the House of Stuart, the Valois of Great Britain. So I will exclude only those two; but the others, all the Cornelis-this, Jan-that, Joris and Peter van den Put or Poters, or something like that . . . unpronounceable peasant names, admit it, and what did they paint? The bourgeois and always the bourgeois, cloth merchants, Beguines, and deputy burgomasters' wives. The Spanish painted kings' daughters, the Italians painted the mistresses of popes, but these good Flemish truly only glorified their companies. Did you visit Haarlem? What Frans Hals! Decidedly the most handsome, but they are still only portraits of officials – worse, they are the national guard of their time. Don't be tricked, Messieurs; the costumes delude you, but if these mustached Flemish have swords by their sides, it is because they are militia leaders, and not gentlemen.

"Civic guards, members of their guild, yes, but noblemen, not at all! And that sword that seduces you and leads you astray, they owe it to the Spanish who conquered them. It is the necessary counterstroke of a whole people in danger, the reply to the scaffold permanently in place in Brussels' Place de l'Hôtel-de-Ville and Antwerp's Place du Marché-aux-Herbes. They had to respond to the Duke of Alba. And then dare to compare these good Dutch colichemardes[†] to the fine swords, decorated with niello or gold damascene, of *The Surrender of Breda* . . . Ah! Velázquez, Messieurs, he is my painter."

Wraithlike and tragic in the half-light of the little museum rooms that were so intelligently arranged, Monsieur de Bougrelon would stop by turns before Rembrandt's *Old Woman* and by one of Gerrit Dou's domestic scenes, arch his back pompously in his Carmelite outfit, and brandish his madly tousled, awful muff at the picture frames, hold forth, lose his temper, sputter; he was silent, he posed, he made theatrical gestures, and suddenly he strode twenty meters across the gallery and became still, rigid as marble on the waxed parquet floor, where reflections of the enormous wheels of his spurs trembled, as though reflected in still water.

"No, Messieurs," he concluded, straightening his long

† A long sword with a large forte narrowing abruptly into a slender foible, similar to a rapier, commonly used for dueling.

chest, "I will not get used to it. These faces of bustards will never appeal to a Bougrelon: a pitiful coat rack to hang the rags of my dreams. But there are better things here than the paintings. Follow me."

Abruptly turning his heels on Rembrandt's *The Night Watch,* he took the staircase on the left to the first-floor galleries, a difficult descent for his old stiff knees, a descent that was even a bit macabre with his rigid, jerky gait of an automaton, a tinny clang with every step – it all made him seem like some exaggerated statue of the Commander[†] on that pale January day.

The stolid, placid attendants watched us pass, and in their tasseled cloaks these good Dutchmen were nearly identical to the unofficial doormen of the Nes's whorehouses.

"I am taking you to the brothel, Messieurs," declared the old puppet, "but the brothel of memories. There you will submit, and with the sharpest desire, to women you will not even see, to a deceptive obsession. I am taking you to the cloakroom of the dead. Standing before scraps of fabric, before dresses that will be empty forever and bodices of nothing, before the old rags of centuries and the tatters of dead lovers, I want to get you drunk on the sorrowful opium of what could have been and what is no more.

Oh! The challenge of an empty bottle, beware

[†] Likely a reference to *Dom Juan ou le Festin de pierre* (*Dom Juan or The Feast with the Statue*), by Molière. The character of the Commander, previously killed by Dom Juan, appears as a statue.

Its perfume, pure and discreet,
Leaving nothing upon our greedy lips
But regret and vain despair!

And, abruptly lifting a door curtain, he went on in a voice that softened strangely: "Prepare yourselves for every suffering. We are in the kingdom of eternal melancholy here. It is a boudoir of ghosts: look at these glass cases. But these ghosts left behind their silk and velvet shrouds, palpable and tangible, to force us to revive them in our memory. We are in a crypt here, but also in a private chapel, a chapel that is quasi-divine, where Christs will rise from their displays if we know how to look; and they will rise precisely because there is nothing magical about these cases, nothing but our regrets and thoughts. There is nothing but rags of silk, of lawn cloth† and brocade, and yet what evocative rags! We will stir up the dust of centuries. There are kisses in this dust, there is madness, there is love, and there are tears. Nostalgic dolls, Messieurs!"

† A fine, light semi-transparent cloth used for blouses, handkerchiefs, and other delicate items.

CHAPTER FIVE

THE BOUDOIR OF THE DEAD

The cloakroom of memory!

In a suite of rooms lit by high windows, display cases after display cases lined the walls, immense armoires of glass like blocks of ice, where the fashions of lost centuries seemed frozen. Touching preserve jars of outmoded elegance, the so-called costume galleries were where the meticulous Dutch guarded the gallant castoffs, dresses, gowns, and jewelry of former queens, shielding them from the dust and humidity. Next to the long pleated robes imitated by Watteau, there were rural scenes by Pater, *gros de Tours* woven with silver fleurs-de-lis upon the Bordeaux-red backdrop of sack-back gowns, delicate striped pekins beside braids of silk, brocades of green myrtle foliage, and glazed satins like rivulets of frost, with Astragalus flowers and love knots, and garlands of blooming carnations and sweet alyssums tied to the fabric with ribbons . . . There was the irritating enigma of bodices puffing out where breasts should have been, and skirts lying flat where stomachs should have been; and there was lampas[†] embossed with great bouquets of red roses upon gold backgrounds, magnificent heavy fabrics that looked as though they were once worn by the wives of big bankers and rich merchants, all the madness of the gold in Amsterdam's banks, all the crushing luxury of the East India Company, the massive opulence befitting the diamond cutting factories' extraordinary profits; it conjured visions of enormous throats *à la* Jordaens and slatterns' hips in satin that was speckled, flaking, inlaid like armor, scattered with half-peeled pomegranates and long pineapples; and then there were, beside green resedas that were fading to sulfur, salmon-pink roses and peach blossoms, all softened and dimmed by the haze of gauzes and lawn cloths; it was the agonizing melancholy of the end of the eighteenth century, tender flax blues and sorrowful lilacs, colors that seemed as though they had been powdered with irises and washed with tears, pastorals of the Trianon displaced to this cold Holland, the romantic daydreams of Jean-Jacques exiled with the nobility of Versailles to the House of Orange, discreet and perfumed strokes of French elegance taking refuge in this country during the Revolution. Alongside the women's finery, there were men's outfits, Louis XV costumes, embroidered and re-embroidered housecoats and court breeches decked with flowers like flower beds, and finally there were long waistcoats of changing hues, sparkling with paste jewels, glistening with sequins, with the necessary

---

[†] A patterned fabric, similar to brocade, made of silk, cotton, or rayon, originally imitating textiles from India. This type of cloth was woven in Europe beginning in the tenth century and was difficult and costly to produce.

strings of daffodils and carnations around the pockets; and we saw crushed velvets that were *bleu de roi* and myrtle green, the jerkins of heroic shepherds, fantastical colors from zinzolin to green celadon, which evoked visions of the long thin torsos of ballet dancers and warrior ephebes, all the pleasures of *The Enchanted Island,* the mythological feasts of Versailles, and masked balls on the frozen ponds of the parks in The Hague.

As we advanced, slowly and contemplatively, along those display cases that were like sarcophagi, an infinite sadness, a tender compassion, penetrated us, wearying and soothing at once; our limbs utterly relaxed, we drifted from here to there, beyond the century, no longer in a museum, but in a sick-room, almost afraid of waking the souls that were in the rags laid out before our eyes.

The Boudoir of the Dead: Monsieur de Bougrelon had found the perfect expression. The old puppet was showing us around a funeral boudoir – pious and flirtatious, it was seductive as an alcove, yet cold as a sacristy. Instinctively we were silent: too many phantoms escorted us; the atmosphere was crowded with them, lying in wait around every corner.

We were now before the coiffures popular at the end of Louis XVI's reign – bold challenges and unexpected whims, they were extravagant, monumental; plumed felt hats swept upon raised piles of hair with straightened roots, colossal crowns of abundant roses around the skullcap of a gigantic Lamballe hat, deep hoods of lawn cloth and silk where a woman's face appeared so deliciously refined in the back of a nook wreathed with flowers.

Monsieur de Bougrelon, who until then had been silent, said, "The enchantment of outdated fashions, the painful charm of bygone things coming alive, Messieurs, do you feel it too? Yes, for I see that you are pale, overcome with an emotion that is so powerful because it is silent. Did I mislead you when I said, 'Prepare yourselves for suffering'? Do you not suffer more from the presence of the adorable dead here, conjured by these few ornaments, than you do before a varnished or lackluster portrait? Oh! The spell of these faded cloths, the patrician languor of all these expertly wrought jewels of silk and satin!

"If a church atmosphere reigns (for do you not feel reverence here, as in a holy place?), it is because the imperious soul of old aristocracies floats here, invisible and palpable. What authoritarian grace, what pride is in the folds of these robes; what innate elegance in these full panniers; what beautiful daring in even the absurdity of these coiffures! I rediscover a whole vanished society here that I once knew. Me, I am at home here. A Boudoir of the Dead, truly, but of the Living Dead, for I know the words that give bodies to these tatters, I know the words of love and tenderness that reawaken smiles and glances here; for these Dead return, yes, Messieurs, these Dead return because I love them, and they obey me because they know: only love resurrects the dead."

And, suddenly leaning on his elbow in the corner of the display cases, in a pose that was both pretentious and inspired, Monsieur de Bougrelon removed his broad sealskin cap with his other hand and said in a theatrical tone:

I am the magnificent lover
Of old faded fabrics.
Outdated fashions and colors,
Who will your spell uncover?

My soul, which suffers and brightens,
Adores the weary smiles
With pink and lilac stripes
Of sulfur-yellow satins;

And it is an exquisite resurrection
To find the blue of a marquise umbrella,
Redolent of carnations and daffodils,
Sparkling in a reflection.

Old lampas like agate under its grime,
Radiant beneath time's sharp nail,
Possess the haughty and delicate
Sadness of a faraway springtime;

Those springs of youth will never come again,
Those cool Aprils blew away,
Whose lilies of thick silks
Shed their petals in grosgrain!

But to sing the intoxication
That rambles through these past luxuries,
These old kisses, these bygone perfumes,

That clever and wounding elation,

You need a basson d'amour[†]
Beneath your docile fingers,
With a long shaft of island wood
Made from a painted chair of Pompadour;

And in the pleasant and devout shadows
Of a boudoir, dark and hidden,
Me, in old-fashioned dress,
Playing rhythmic gavotte tempos,

I would summon the spirit, fallen behind,
Of old faded fabrics,
And the sweet, dreamy enchantment
Of colors, forever refined!

"Old perfumes, old kisses, old lampas, faraway spring-times, rhythmic gavotte melodies, old painted Dresden por-celain, luxuries forever abolished, yes, all of that is my youth, my youth in old-fashioned dress, withered as I myself am now. An old dandy forgotten in a century of money and gross appetites, an old puppet who has taken refuge amongst phan-toms: that is truly what I am, Messieurs."

He stopped, short of breath. His makeup was running down his cheeks; two thin blackish rivulets of water appeared

[†] An instrument similar to the baroque bassoon, played during the eighteenth and early nineteenth centuries, usually to accompany church psalms.

at his temples, and two others at the corners of his lips (the cosmetics of his mustache and his eyebrows); and, cadaverous beneath the slurry of his red and white makeup, utterly exhausted, falling to pieces, his energy sapped in the suddenly too-large folds of his breeches, Monsieur de Bougrelon, emptier and more wrecked than even the ornaments of nothing on display all around him, was indeed the pitiful lover of faded fabrics, the macabre and debauched gentleman of that funeral boudoir.

An old scarecrow to put in the fields to scare birds, that is what our noble and dignified guide through the splendors of the Rijksmuseum was.

We took pity on his decrepitude. We sat him down almost forcefully on a bench, and, having mopped up his sweat with our handkerchiefs, we tried to galvanize the poor old cadaver with salts, not without the secret anxiety of seeing him liquefy in our arms. It would have been too dreadful to witness his death throes in that Boudoir of the Dead. Monsieur de Bougrelon was worn out. From the emotion or the fatigue of having pontificated for so long, his upper body swayed in silence, propped up between us, and, his lip dangling, he let his lifeless eyes roam over the display cases, where just a while earlier so much madness and so many lost loves had beat their wings and whispered, coming back to life for him.

Eleven o'clock. The carillon of the old church filled the long museum rooms with a thin glasschord[†] melody: the

---

[†] An early instrument that uses keyboard-driven hammers to strike glass bars. Sometimes called a glass harmonica. Similar to a celesta, with a sweeter sound.

vitrines vibrated.

"Eleven o'clock! But for my stomach it's noon," thundered Monsieur de Bougrelon, suddenly waking from his slump. "I will take you to lunch, Messieurs. I know a certain sailors' tavern nearby where you will eat Zeeland oysters that are white and fat like girls, and marinated herring as they only make it in Groningen. A thousand apologies for having alarmed you with my blackout. I am prone to them when Barbara speaks to me, and Barbara, I should have told you, always speaks to me in the Boudoir of the Dead. Follow me, Messieurs?"

We followed the old suitor's footsteps. Suddenly revived, his back more arched than ever, as though energized by the biting cold outside, Monsieur de Bougrelon led the way, going wherever his fancy took him, and, incorrigible, he hummed to a gavotte melody:

I am the magnificent lover
Of old faded fabrics.

CHAPTER SIX

IMAGINARY PLEASURES

"Yes, Messieurs, the fog of this country induces strange fantasies. I already mentioned the case of Lady Barbara van Mierris to you. Hers is one of the most bizarre cases; but have some more of this haddock. Have you ever tasted fish like this? It is so milky, and so fresh! A person can eat wonderfully in this sailors' tavern, eh? Didn't I tell you so?"

The sailors' tavern where Monsieur de Bougrelon had taken us was a clean, glowing ocean liner's cabin that was installed, for some unknown reason, in the basement cellar of a wood shack on the North Sea quay; all the way at the edge of the city, behind the Centraal Station and the warehouses, facing the steamboats that were getting ready to depart for the Zuiderzee and New Holland, there was an entire wharf of temporary structures, boathouses, and travelers' restaurants with makeshift roofs of tar-covered planks, with stacks of crates and pyramids of barrels sitting directly on the road, waiting to be loaded, and, from place to place, the narrow progress of jetties, their stilt floors extending into the yellowish gray of the North Sea.

It was truly a landscape of infinite melancholy, this Port Entrepôt, with its cobblestones hardened by the frost and its sporadic buildings that had turned black in the dust and smoke of ocean liners, its melancholy even further heightened by the solitude of the docks and jetties, for the lunch hour had emptied all of Westel's storehouses. In the distance, the sea extended for miles and miles – the color of hemp and pewter, a restless sea that stirred beneath an eternal bitter kiss that made it alternately gray and yellow, but always pale. On the horizon, there was the Tolhuistuin, with its denuded trees, and the Noordzeekanaal, a long parallelogram of unchanging pallor that had been carved out of the earth.

"Three months of vacation by this monotonous sea, and the soul, weakened by ennui, Messieurs, is ripe for the worst debauchery. This country of fog and humidity predisposes you to everything, and the ugliness of the residents helps too; because, between us, the types you see here have superhuman looks: gourds and melons, Messieurs, those are their silhouettes. As for their coloring, they are eggplants. Their skin chapped with cold, the Dutch are a people of violet cheeks. Each people, by the way, takes the color of some fruit: Spain has the hue of an orange, feverish Italy is green as an olive, and the French woman is as downy-pink as a peach. I myself have always thought of women like fruit. Fie on bland comparisons to flowers: the flower is gathered, the fruit is eaten, and Monsieur de Mortimer and I always salivated at the idea of standing before a table set with girls' corsets.

"Besides, there are women who suddenly become ogress-es before the nakedness of young men – Barbara was one of these. We met her, Monsieur de Mortimer and I, in Haarlem, at the house of an old tulip collector who had invited us to see his plants; Holland is crazy about horticulture. White and fat with two fleshy nipples, which were smooth as milk and always displayed in the opening of her bodice of embossed damask, with her big strong hips swathed in panniers of heavy fabrics, her legs entangled in long rustling trains, in her collarettes and cherusque collars of malines[†] and gold lace, with her strings of pearls around her neck, a ferronnière on her forehead, and a thousand and one baubles as pendants on her breasts and ears, she was a Rubens woman in every sense of the word, a display case and a butcher's stall. Her neck, with its three folds, was so plump and so round, her earlobes so crimson, her skin so transparent, and her small teeth so pearly white between the moist pink of her lips, that you would have wanted to eat this woman with a spoon, Messieurs, like a sorbet . . . She was tasty and glazed with sug-ar, or at least appeared to be.

"The widow of a great Rotterdam shipowner, she was kept for a long time, or so they said, by a prince of the House of Orange,[‡] and she lived on a canal in a sumptuous home made of three gabled houses, furnished with all the oppressive lux-ury and sturdy pomp of the interiors of this country. She

[†] A delicate net resembling tulle, originally made by hand in Mechlin, Belgium.

[‡] The Dutch royal house, originally a princely dynasty of the principality centered on the town of Orange in the sixteenth century.

truly did want to do us the honors – Monsieur de Mortimer was hungry for whiskey-perfumed almond milk, and almond milk and whiskey, that was precisely her flesh – but this frankly barbarian Barbara always fought off his advances with a resistance that was as firm as her breasts, which were like two strongholds.

"Dear Edgard got little for his advances, and I got little for my own, and we never knew the snowy kiss of those crimson lips, for that damned Dutch woman's breath was all frost, Monsieur. When we breathed her in, it was like a hedge of wild roses in bloom, but mountain roses halfway up the side of a glacier. This Hollander never smelled the swamp. Monsieur de Mortimer and I were with her for our short-lived humiliation, though short is a bold understatement, Messieurs, because our desire was great.

"For two years we did not understand the enigma of her chastity. Barbara had no lover, and if her heart had to decide, her choice would have fallen (she told us so herself) between Mortimer and me, for she strongly appreciated both of us. Oh, the exasperating mystery of that sorbet that never melted!

The irritating insult of sleet
That does not thaw,
The haughty peaks that withdraw
Beyond the reach of our feet.

"We discovered the key to this mystery of innocence and sensuality one day by penetrating the secrets of her bathtub.

This soul of snow hardened herself in the fire of desire, and, to guard her rigidity, baked herself in the furnace of the most formidable lust: the lust of a Negro. Lady Barbara van Mierris bathed every morning before a colossal Ethiopian. With a refinement of carnal cruelty, this white ogress (she really was one) had placed an enormous African in her team of intimate domestics, yes, Messieurs, a giant Negro who yearned for her with the most frantic, burning desires. She made him lace her up and put on her shoes; it was he who helped her out of the bath and sponged her down in her swan's down robes, but prudently he wore leather undergarments, and in these martyr's trunks, the captive man pined away, his dreadful desire sheathed in a jail. It was in this atmosphere of the most torturous lust that the blond and fat Hollander blossomed and fortified herself against our advances. She lived, hungry for emotion, in perpetual fear of rape and pleased herself by observing that eternal threat. Meanwhile, the simple child of the desert, with his concupiscence always aroused and always threatening her like a firebrand, was indeed the black statue of insatiable Desire . . . A bronze statue, Messieurs, whose every look and every gesture made metal vibrate, and which she turned into a bell clapper within her ivory tower, the ivory tower where she lived shut away, guarded by this desire so hostile to our own, a monstrous pendulum of the clock of her chastity.

"Imaginary pleasure, Messieurs, as only this cloudy country's atmosphere of dreams and fog can produce! Incidentally, this perpetual attack on an inaccessible, proffered modesty ended with crime. The incessant torture of Tantalus drove the tempted Negro so mad that one evening the beast within the child of the desert roared awake. One does not play with tigers and leave unscathed . . . Lady Barbara van Mierris was found strangled in her bathtub one morning, Messieurs, with an enormous gaping wound on her neck and one of her breasts bitten, torn apart, half-devoured, bloody. The Negro, rabid with lust, had treated her like a fruit, and then the culprit fled. But the unsullied cadaver (you understand what I mean), although mutilated, was not the only victim. Before killing his pretty mistress, the Ethiopian had strangled Lady Barbara's macaw and favorite guenon monkey with his murderous hands – two charming animals, the guenon especially, which was almost human in its ugliness and simpering manner. The best trained of all her companions, the tame guenon acted as a chambermaid to the blond Dutch woman. Paquita was its name, and this lady-monkey was a character, Messieurs, sometimes decked out in yellow satin, sometimes in orange moiré and golden velvet, in a deep bodice fastened by large ribbons to form a wasp waist, with great sleeve flounces at her elbows like a marquise; seeing her, Mortimer and I were often troubled, for this guenon demonstrated the charms and flirtatiousness of a woman. Divinely made up, with blush on her cheeks and kohl around her eyes, the guenon was more than a doll for Barbara: she was a child, a friend, *the little heart* passionately cherished by that truly extraordinary Dutch woman, who seemed to prefer black to white, animal to man, temperament of ice to abnormal desires.

"But why should I emphasize this any more? You have understood me, Messieurs. Even slanderers do not dare to utter the word that we all whispered, why the Negro strangled that guenon. The parrot – a white macaw with pink-stained wings and a beak gilded with ormolu (Barbara had an inconceivably refined sense of luxury) – had the dubious habit of pecking at the lips of its lady and would not eat except from her mouth, as it had been trained to do . . . Paquita, she styled and unstyled the Dutch woman's hair night and day . . . Jealousy armed the Negro's hand, but I will say no more about it: we must respect the dead, and I, for five years, passionately loved this mad Barbara.

"This ginger jam, Messieurs, has no comparison in all of Holland. It comes here directly from Java."

Monsieur de Bougrelon, casually tilting back in his chair, had brought out from the depths of his breeches a powder box, cosmetics, a comb, and a pocket mirror of carved silver; my word, it was a curious piece, with pink topazes and moonstones set here and there in the metal. "This mirror is quite pretty, isn't it? With its lunar setting, like a twilight moon. These pink topazes and selenites, are they not the rising of Diana in the setting sun? It came from Barbara, Messieurs. It was her guenon's mirror."

And, without deigning to notice the crazed laughter that burst from us at this connection, the old imperturbable beau powdered his cadaver's face; with rouge he brightened the pinched nostrils of his aquiline nose, his dry thin lips, the parchment of his cheeks; he made the stiff points of his mustache sticky with cosmetics, revived his eyebrows and the bags of his lashless eyes with black pencil, patched up his old ruined face, replenished his ancient beauty with ointments.

Outside there was cold and ice, the frosted-glass sky of misty Holland, the stirring North Sea waves the color of hemp and pewter . . .

"Imaginary pleasure, Messieurs! Imaginary pleasure!"

CHAPTER SEVEN

FANTASTIC MUFF

"This seething, bewildering, intellectual lust is Flemish, par-
ticular to these northern souls – it pierces instinct and breaks
through to the other side of species and sex. Holland does
not have a monopoly on it; Belgium is ravaged by it too,
Messieurs, and without dwelling too long on the orgiastic
paintings of the Antwerp School . . . .
(and the bawdiness of Teniers' street festivities, which I might
forget!), I will say that this ravage extends even to Bruges-the-
Holy – Bruges, that reliquary of ivory and gold, where the
pewter of canals reflects precious illuminations by Van Eyck
and Memling – even to Bruges – that Bruges that people say
is dead,[†] but which is only asleep – where, swathed in mystic
linens, the most titillating obscenity is coddled, that of the
Beguines!

"Have you visited Bruges? And in Bruges, the bells of its
belfry? . . . It is a dormitory of nuns, Messieurs, bronze nuns,
which the belfry rings for prayers. For those kneeling vir-

† Reference to Georges Rodenbach's 1892 novel *Bruges-la-Morte*.

gins, the chimes are their litanies. Even when they are silent, they are the murmuring urns of dreams, for they are spirits, Messieurs. Yes, they were baptized, and the carillonneur – who puts this group in motion and makes the prayer of their metal flesh gush forth – is their confessor, never their lover. But in Bruges-the-Holy, there is indeed a man, a Belgian, a Fleming, who desires and demands the love of those bronze bells: the fact is historic, Messieurs! In Bruges they told us his name.

"An unprecedented case of imaginary pleasure, which will perhaps inspire a future novelist, this Boorluut (for his name has just come back to me) loved the bells like they were girls, like working girls, Messieurs, and took the same sensual and carnal delight in swinging them that you or I take in screwing tarts, so much so that the belfry of Bruges became a vessel of lust, and the chimes of those guilty bells ended by corrupting the city. The bells trembled with desire – with rut! – till, as Monsieur de Mortimer would say, it is not Boorluut, but Horrut that this bold straddler of bronze rumps should have been called.

"This story, Messieurs, will not be an excuse in your eyes, but it will at least make it easier for you to understand the strange adventure that Monsieur de Mortimer and I let ourselves slip into, even here in Holland. We did not love any bells, no, but our lust, as imaginary as it was, will perhaps seem worse to you. You be the judge, once you have heard to what extremes two magnanimous souls can ascend to or descend to when they are ravaged by ennui, by fierce ennui,

ennui that scathes like acid, ennui, a ring of lead that puts the eternal weight of this gray, dismal sky upon your temples. Yes, the mist of Holland truly leads to strange fantasies." And, curling his stiff dyed mustache with the proud, nonchalant, lovely gesture of a king's musketeer, he went on, "I already told you, Messieurs, how dear Barbara van Mierris was to us. White, fat, and as silvery blond as the Spanish infantas or a pedigree spaniel, this divine woman possessed, along with many other charms, the incomparable appeal of two liquid green eyes; but not emerald green, no, her eyes were absinthe green, whipped absinthe actually, a green that was as milky and transparent as a peridot. Those eyes – whoever has not known them does not know the color of potions. It was a potion, Messieurs, and a black potion, a potion of shadows, the eyes of Astarte, the very look of lust, which I often saw in my dreams, glowing in the plaster pupils of Antinous.

"We adored Barbara when she was alive! So you can imagine how we idolized her when she was dead . . . ! During the cold winter days, as Monsieur de Mortimer and I walked, exiled, in an incurable state of ennui along the frozen canals or these deserted quays, eyes would flutter before us, like nostalgic will-o'-the-wisps, eyes of transparent, glaucous water, belonging to that most desirable woman in Holland . . .

"Well, one January morning, when Mortimer and I were trying to distract ourselves from our melancholy, we decided to go to the island of Marken to scratch the hard ice with our skates. (About that, Messieurs, you must visit this island. The women's outfits are delicious there. Like me, you will love their short scarlet skirts and their Diana's legs in gaiters, and on top of that, the gold antennae pointing out from under their halo headdresses; those truly epic headdresses, half-Japanese and half-Flemish, will make your liver swell with delight. In Beguine cornettes and samurai helmets, these fisherwomen of Marken are all little Salomes, with their short petticoats and glistening diadems; red as lady apples, Messieurs, they have firm breasts and eyes of saltwater. Oh! This island has good things, and I do not pity its fishermen.) So we wandered, Monsieur de Mortimer and I, over the quays of Monnickendam (Monnickendam is the port of departure for Marken). We ate a lunch of salt cod, potato mash, and bustard in anchovy butter, renowned dishes of the region, and we ambled along the quays, as I told you, a bit disappointed because of the heavy ice floes in the port. At first we thought we would be able to reach Marken by ice skating; an error, Messieurs, for the ice was not hard enough, and anyway, the sea swept along so many floes that it would have been madness to risk a small boat. Anyway, no fisherman would have lent us his bark. It was thus postponed, and, as the true Frenchmen that we were, we sulked – and with what dour looks! – over this stroke of bad luck, when suddenly Barbara's eyes of green water lit up before us . . . Those eyes, they were her eyes, and we weren't drunk on *Schiedammer* either (it was only two o'clock); those eyes stared at us; even better, those eyes smiled at us, defying us, Messieurs; and those eyes (you will tremble when I tell you) were the eyes of a dog, of a ghastly street cur, a white poodle filthy with soot and coal . . . It was not even a spaniel, a delicious King Charles as Landseer painted, one of those delectable creatures of luxury all covered in locks of silver-blond silk, that silver-blond that the living Barbara used to wear in her blond-silver hair; no, it was a pitiful and squalid poodle, though beneath its tangled fur there was the magnet of two liquid green eyes, so glaucous and phospho-rescent green that . . . without saying a word, Monsieur de Mortimer and I exchanged a look – and what a look! – that so frightened the green-eyed poodle that it bolted. We followed it; it sped ahead of us, sheepish, its tail between its legs; we followed it, we even chased it. Oh! The fog of Holland has a terrible influence on exiled souls! . . . We forced the beast past the outskirts of the city. 'I sense a Negro's soul,' Monsieur de Mortimer said to me then. Good Lord, that was clear. The terrified poodle fixed two great supplicant eyes on us; sadly, they were like two green almonds, the color of a reed or a young sprout.

"We took the unfortunate creature to a hairdresser, Mes-sieurs, who lathered her with soap, bathed her, perfumed her with bergamot and *eau de Portugal,* and, after many sham-pooings (for a trifling ten florins!), delivered her, curled and fragrant of a thousand flowers, the most delicious white poodle (and thankfully a female) that any duchess-peeress painted by Gainsborough could have dreamed of for her foot cushion . . . Enthused, Monsieur de Mortimer immediately bought her a turquoise collar and named her Barbara.

"It is her fur that I wear," Monsieur de Bougrelon sudden-ly burst forth (he had risen violently), "but her fur stained

black in mourning, for I will not hide from you that the canine Barbara had a bloody end: her name predestined that.
Barbara was murdered, she had to be murdered, and out of
jealousy just like the Other. Monsieur de Mortimer was her
Negro. She reminded him too much of that woman who had
made him suffer, and so the present avenged the past. One
day, he could no longer tolerate the haunting illusion of her
eyes, and he cut the unfortunate poodle's neck . . . unfortunate and innocent. I had this muff made, Messieurs, from her
bloody fur, dyed black . . . I used to think about carelessly
throwing into these long dark locks two peridots, two pale
emeralds that could have reminded me of her look, but that
would have been too morbid a lust, and anyway, I later found
her phosphorescent and murky look, her diabolically green
pupils, that nostalgic glaucous potion, in the soul of Atala."[†]

We were dealing with a madman. This time, Monsieur de
Bougrelon had exceeded moderation: Monsieur de Bougrelon
had gone too far. He did not say much more that day. Our host
rose; we had already been at the table for five hours, and, in
the mist, the occasional streetlamps were beginning to come
on along the quays. It was the hour when his well-wishing noblewoman awaited the old exile of Avranches. Every night, he
dined at this beautiful woman's home and played ombre with
her. All of the old gentleman's nights belonged to this loyal
friend, to his companion through hard times . . . So Monsieur
de Bougrelon rose, put his hat on, turned up his beribboned

[†] Reference to the novella *Atala, ou Les Amours de deux sauvages dans le desert* (1801)
by François-René de Chateaubriand.

collar, and, with a haughty salute of his fingertips, took his leave of us.

As usual, he left it to us to settle the bill.

On the doorstep, he said, "You will not see me tomorrow, Messieurs. I regret leaving you in the lurch. But I will be at my devotions all day, at Mass and Vespers at my Dutch woman's private chapel, the one who occupies my evenings. Tomorrow is Sunday after all. Until Monday then, Messieurs."

Like a phantom, dizzying and macabre, this extraordinary man pirouetted and *pfft!*, evaporated into the shadows of the great deserted quay . . . It was nothing short of miraculous. One would have thought he had fallen into the night.

The next day was dreary. Oh! The sadness of Sundays abroad!

We went back to the museum, visited the Fodor collection[†] (whose outdated name was truly the only thing that pleased us), and around five o'clock, as we were meandering through the narrow, busy alleys of the Zeedijk (in the marine quarter), amused by the dives whose horn windows were lighting up one by one as night was falling, we thought we saw, at the corner of one of those streets, slipping away, careful and sly, the green redingote of our guide. Oh! It was no longer the beautiful, impertinent, and aggressive allure of the Bougrelon we knew. He had nothing of the great leading man, nothing of the Capitano of two days before, not this poor old fellow with the sliding, furtive walk, his head sunk between his shoulders,

---

[†] In 1860, Carl Joseph Fodor bequeathed to the city of Amsterdam his collection of paintings and drawings, which were housed in the Museum Fodor until 1993.

who hastened his step as he went along the walls, as though trying to look so small that he would not be seen. No, it could not be him; the barely glimpsed silhouette carried some kind of parcel in a slipcover under his arm, an oblong package like musicians carry when they are going to play in the city; a long instrument handle, as of a violin or guitar, pointed out of the package. And the man was not alone. An old woman wrapped up in a great shawl dragged herself along after him, painfully bent beneath the weight of a harp; they were a couple of poor traveling musicians. We had obviously made a mistake . . . Anyway, soon the man and woman were pressed against a wall; barely visible for a moment, they vanished, as though they had fallen through a cellar window . . . and we felt the jolt of a new suspicion at this brusque disappearance, at this phantom vanishing, so similar to the spectral exits of Monsieur de Bougrelon; but in life there are the strangest similarities, the most disturbing encounters. We continued our sluggish tour of the dives of the Zeedijk, amused by our mistake, even a bit intrigued by our hypothesis, which would not have displeased us if it were true.

CHAPTER EIGHT

VISIONS OF ART

On Monday, Monsieur de Bougrelon did not turn up. We moped around for two hours without seeing his terrifying silhouette appear in the hotel lobby.

So, battle weary, we decided to take an excursion to Zaandam, for one must follow travel guides, and a day in Zaandam is mentioned everywhere, along with a visit to the Czaar Peterhuisje; but how to make yourself understood in this cursed dialect, half-English and half-German, that they babble in Holland! . . . With our inexperience in the language, it was a true problem, and it was such a hardship to obtain the necessary information that we missed our steamboat's departure by ten minutes.

We would have had to wait for an hour on that harsh Port Entrepôt, exposed to the winds, which blew and whistled that day on the Noordzeekanaal. Those waves, the color of hemp and pewter, had never been rougher, and the melancholy of that region of dreams and fog had never been more poignant. Oh! That day we felt the gloomy, the incurably depressing, sensation of exile . . . We missed our usual spokesman. Amsterdam was not Amsterdam anymore without Monsieur de Bougrelon. He was the raison d'être of that wintry, indistinct setting of frozen canals and black-and-white gabled houses; he was its gaiety and its fantasy; and it was through the excess of his heroic visions that we had loved the monotony of its streets and the genuinely hostile ugliness of its inhabitants. This hostility had never offended us as much as it did that day. In our distress, we amused ourselves by repeating the phrases our missed companion had used the day before to denounce this ugliness.

"Gourds and melons, those are the silhouettes, Messieurs, with eggplant complexions; their skin chapped with cold, the Dutch are a people of violet cheeks. As for the types you meet, bundled up in furs and topped with woolly hats, they are seals! Yes, they vary, Messieurs, between dried fish and sea calves. Their main street Kalverstraat means the Street of Calves, and they do it justice, for they are calves, Messieurs." It was not that these remarks showed a certain unrest, but that day their exaggeration pleased us. It validated our weariness and revived our souls, exhausted by ennui. We decided to leave that very night, but resolved to return to Haarlem before that to see the Frans Hals paintings again. That would be the task of the day, and we would come back to pack our suitcases at nightfall.

Yet we had barely arrived at the station when a fine rain began to fall, and the showers followed us. The rain wove a humid darkness on our carriage windows; it drowned the landscape of phantom windmills and fields of dry reeds with water: it was the saddest expedition. We found Haarlem to be dour in the rain, a Haarlem of empty streets and dripping-wet windows beneath a sky of soot, dissolving in torrential showers.

A sumptuous carriage, official down to the coachman's livery, carted us from museum to museum to the Stadhuis, the age-old treasure chest of Haarlem; but beneath the incessant rain drumming against the windows and pattering on the roof tiles, the Frans Hals paintings left us rather cold. In the pallid aquarium light, too clean and too polished, all the aldermen and civic watchmen were like *objets d'art,* caressing our eyes without becoming real; they were missing the prestigious cicerone Monsieur de Bougrelon would have been. We ate poorly in a sort of tavern located across from the Saint Bavo "Lutheran cathedral," as our missed guide would have said, "whose empty look and frozen nudity numb the soul." In that tavern we sustained ourselves on lukewarm food, as weak and bland as the landscape; the sauces were colorless, the fish boneless, and the meat bloodless; only the ginger jam cheered us up, but, to wipe our hands, we had a puzzling abundance of paper napkins, and the plates were of old Delft pottery marked with slogans, with French words, no less:

Bonjour, monsieur, bonjour.

A strange country, where the plates speak like parrots![†]

The fish market, with its fishwives wearing top hats upon

[†] The plates may be *faïence parlante,* which bear mottoes often on decorative labels or banners.

lace caps, demanded some of our time. The fish shops are marvelous in the Netherlands – every stall, with its merchandise of mother-of-pearl and quicksilver, is a picture – and so that was our day in Haarlem, where we did not see any tulips.

Rain fell the whole time; we found it again in Amsterdam, where we returned earlier than we had anticipated: an hour in Haarlem has one hundred and twenty minutes, and one must sometimes cut it short.

Amsterdam was lighting up as we arrived. In the presence of the radiant shop windows, the gaslights at the street corners, and the electric lighthouse beacons, our weariness dissipated. Kalverstraat teemed with the comings and goings of chubby Dutch men and overjoyed Dutch women, lumbering along with large rumps and powerful waists beneath the pattering rain; it excited us, and, beginning to regain our zest for life, we sauntered – amused and curious flâneurs – before the blazing fashion shop displays and the diamond merchants' windows.

In the midst of all these dazzling things, we stopped in front of a sumptuous shop of furs and travel goods, which the Dutch have refined. It displayed handbags and *nécessaires,* with exquisite ornaments of nickel and silver that bit directly into the tan of sows' hides or the velvety gray of the softest deer skins. There were also suitcases, like works of art, under blurs of belts and fine steel buckles, with so much choice in the hues and the grains of the leathers that this window display became a disconcerting and tender vision, an immediate request for intimate contact, for sly petting. An impression of nudity stood out so strongly in it; the half-open dives of the Nes were less suggestive of the intoxication of flesh . . . The furs, martens, minks, and sables thrown across objects only made them more obscene; those silky shadows of blond and brown locks looked like shaved heads of hair, like pubic fleece, perverse yet discreet strokes upon these naked skins; and all these furs and fawny leathers tempted, caressed, accosted.

"Do you have Negro souls? Ah, I discover you here, Messieurs. You too are under its influence – the noxious influence of this depressing country of mist. Imaginary pleasures. They flash before your eyes, tremble in your hands, manifest themselves in your whole feverish attitude. Monsieur de Mortimer and I had those same penetrating blue pupils in Monnickendam as we hunted the unfortunate white poodle, which I wore the other day, its fur now a muff."

Monsieur de Bougrelon had suddenly appeared behind us, we did not know how or from where, as was his fiendish custom, a Monsieur de Bougrelon who was shiny, polished, painted, and newly replastered, his cheeks pink and his mustache waxed, a Monsieur de Bougrelon who was corseted, with his back arched and his nose turned up, wearing a black velvet spencer like a German student. His long old eagle's neck emerged from a lather of shabby red lace; green and blue precious stones were carelessly jabbed into his collar – faux sapphires and faux emeralds (because real ones would have cost the old puppet ten thousand florins) that completed the adornment of a perfect charlatan.

Holding a muscadin's pince-nez at eye level in his right

hand, Monsieur de Bougrelon smiled, lazily leaning into his right hip; his crossed legs were like a pedestal for his bust. He rested with his other hand on an enormous, gold-knobbed twisted cane, a token of *executive power,* as Vernet's figures carry, and indeed the heroic silhouette of Monsieur de Bougrelon embodied a Vernet that day, under the pouring rain.

"And you would be foolish, Messieurs, and worse, impotent, to resist the hairy, soft, and tickling charm of these tawny, supple leathers, exacerbated by these furs. How tempting is this display, Messieurs! In France you would not stop here – there are Frenchwomen to see in the street – but here, the humid atmosphere and the oblique light envelop things so tenderly that the objects are lubricated by them. These bags and furs – why, they are the whole Dutch School! There are no still lifes here, for the still lifes are alive! Do you understand Monsieur de Mortimer now?"

And a bit embarrassed (for some people had begun to gather around us), we gave the impression that we were going to leave; but the old madman pointed to a travel throw with the end of his club, a beige cloth lined with I-do-not-know-what unknown fur, all of long, silky, silvery locks that were as silver-blond as a spaniel's ears. "Barbara's hair, Messieurs! It had this color and fluffiness." And he pointed out a Tibetan goatskin with his pince-nez: "Barbara's very coat, Messieurs, Barbara the poodle, the Other. Do you see the connection now? The obvious reminder of identical sensations between these two objects? Two objects – but no, I express myself badly, two beings. For there are no objects in Holland. There are only visions. It seems people are eavesdropping . . . The peasants do us this honor. We need a change of scenery, Messieurs – we have drawn enough people to this place. The French taste rules here: this merchant's fortune is made as long as we stay in front of his window." Then, slipping his arm familiarly under my own, Monsieur de Bougrelon led us away from Kalverstraat.

"A *Schiedammer,* are you in the mood for a *Schiedammer,* Messieurs? I have two hours to give you before my rendez-vous, as you know, at my lady's house . . . My *dame de beauté,* whom I truly must present you to one of these evenings. She has the most unusual collection of preserves."

"Preserves?" we balked.

"Exactly, preserves, because here preserves, Messieurs, are true visions of art. I have seen *chinois*[†] and apricot jars that would make Van Ostade turn pale. Only Rubens, or rather only Van Dyck, could fight with the pink flesh and silver sheen of certain anchovy bottles. And the marinated oysters, Messieurs! With their ragged and ashen look, these decom-posing shreds (one might even say fetuses), oh, what a poem! These bottles of oysters contain all of Goya's *Sabbaths.* They are stillborn infants offered by sorcerers to Mamouth,[‡] king of the demons. And I will not belabor the green *phallika*[§] evoked

[†] Small green oranges preserved in brandy.

[‡] Likely a reference to Moloch, also spelled Molech, a Canaanite deity associated in biblical sources with the practice of child sacrifice.

[§] French, *phallophories.* The ancient Greek *phallika* were processions in honor of Dionysus in which celebrants carried a large phallus.

by asparagus jars. What a reliquary of memories for a courtesan! And then there are the citrons, the round glass towers where, like silk stuffing, plump citrons sleep in heaps! . . . Ah! Those firm citrons, sweet-smelling, flavorful, at once breasts and peaches, fruit and flesh – it is in the Boudoir of the Dead, before the bodices that will be empty forever in the costume gallery, that one should savor these one by one.

"Imaginary delicacies, yes, Messieurs, and the wonderful colors, the yellow, green, and murky blue radiance of the preserves – they are so many visions of art! I told you already and will repeat it: you will find the most spellbinding nostalgia in jars of fruits and vegetables . . . Vegetables first, what a source of the fantastic! The old Flemish painters understood this well when they introduced into their anatomies of devils and their compositions of monsters, into their *Sabbaths* and their *Temptations,* all the fruits and vegetables of creation. You remember the Hieronymus Bosch in the museum in Brussels; try to call back your memories, recollect the painting of the great battle of the angels and demons. The worst spirits are depicted there, some by leeks, another by a winged turnip like a bee, that equal all your phantasmagorical vipers and dragons; and the famous frog with his half-open stomach, showing his insides of pomegranate, what an unexpected horror, what a comical abomination! Because they are works of art, this terror and horror can become seductive and charming, and this seduction, this attraction even, you will submit to, even you, when you visit my lady's collection. You burned like twigs in front of this store just now. I am sure of you –

you will be touched by the soul of Atala."

"The soul of Atala?"

CHAPTER NINE

THE SOUL OF ATALA

"The soul of Atala was a pineapple, Messieurs, a pineapple bathed in its own juice, a pineapple in a preserving jar, but what a pineapple! What a jar! And what juice! When Monsieur de Mortimer and I discovered it in a grocer's window in the Dam, we suddenly felt the innermost reaches of our souls flooded with light, the innermost reaches of our hearts bathed in ecstasy . . . This jar gleamed, like an enormous emerald with a golden-palmed fruit frozen inside it . . . This pineapple, Messieurs, was Barbara's eyes and the depths of the sea.

"Vertiginous and glaucous, it contained the whole Atlantic Ocean, Messieurs, and the whole Pacific, and all the Indies and America too. It was some indescribable, transparent green vision, soaked in shadows and sun, a reremembered vision that had navigated past algae, glints of light, and masts, swaying algae, fallen masts, and lost glints, *the depths of the ocean,* as I already said. All the sorrow, all the regret of planned departures, of aborted dreams, of unfulfilled joys, floated in that jar. Nostalgic and mysterious, it was a place of reverie, haunted by specters and debris; there were ancient shipwrecks and ghosts of dead lovers in it. The pineapple leaves, like slow green pendulums, and the pineapple itself, grimacing and frozen behind the glass, came to life there, and in those shadows became so many strange creatures that immobile life disturbs.

"This jar was an abyss, Messieurs! And better than that, the abyss, the Abyss and its rippling virescent nightmare, the abyss imprisoned behind walls of glass, the soul of voyages, the soul of faraway countries, of the Americas and the distant Indies, the soul of Java, Sumatra, and the Happy Isles,[†] the islands that you never reach; in short, the soul of Atala (for this name evokes them all) captivates with its chasm within the seeming banality of a preserving jar. Why, it was all the loftiness of '*L'Invitation au voyage*,' all of Baudelaire in a shopkeeper's window!

"Voilà! That is what this pineapple was, Messieurs.

"Monsieur de Mortimer and I did not hesitate – we never hesitated, even in front of poodles. We went into that grocer's shop and we bought that jar.

"For a long time it decorated the sumptuous home that Mortimer and I made our place of suffering, a stone's throw away from the Admiral de Ruyter Hotel, in the wind and fog of the Prins Hendrikkade . . . A delightful retreat, Messieurs, a lodging that we vastly improved, and especially Mortimer, with his luxuries and studies of art, cultivated with the taste of a gentleman – and he was, more of a gentleman than any-

† Likely a reference to the poem "Ulysses" (1842) by Lord Alfred Tennyson. "It may be we shall touch the Happy Isles, / And see the great Achilles, whom we knew."

one in the world. He was the last one, and I truly regret that you did not know him. He would have charmed you. You would have been lured by the birdlime of his manners. He had proud and charming manners, and simply watching him walk, stand up, and sit down, without him even opening his mouth, would have been a bath of delights, a marvel of elegance and beautiful living that your grandsons, Messieurs, will never imagine.

"My dear Edgard! He spent five years of his youth in London, and it was so obvious that he knew Brummel, King George, and Buckingham. He was, truthfully, one of the only men of the century, and if my heart is bursting with regret as I think of the friend that I lost, I am proud, Messieurs, to have been his companion in exile, the fearless and loyal Patroclus to that Norman with the profile of Achilles."

He poured a new glass of *Schiedammer.*

"He was full of charming anecdotes. He lived most of them. The society we moved around in was not exactly the gathering of oafs that it is today. Would you like an example? The papers these days make such a hubbub when financiers organize hunts. They are the noblemen of our time. This is a pitiful era, Messieurs, and how much more pitiful is this society for which money is everything.

"And indeed, when Monsieur de Mortimer and I hunted deer in mid-autumn (deer or wild boar, for we were formidable hunters) at Vidame Gondrecourt's, whose income was rather paltry (barely sixty thousand) and whose nobility was actually quite recent (these Gondrecourts dated from

81

Louis XII) – do you know how guests were treated in this little lordship in Poitou? For morning hunts, at four o'clock sharp, twenty tailors' apprentices, twenty seamstresses, twenty little Poitou girls fresh as lady apples, twenty of the city's dressmakers invaded the guest rooms and, so swift with their nimble hands, with thimbles on their fingers and threads in their mouths, sewed us as we stood into our leather breeches. They covered us stitch by stitch in buffed deerskin, so hastily that they sometimes pricked us in the behind, and we were so stiff in our breeches that, like picadors, it sometimes took two men to plant us in a saddle.

"After an hour's riding we were flexible, but so bloody in our buckskins, with our legs so glued to the sides of our mounts, that we became one, us, our breeches, and our stallion!

"And what a hunt, Messieurs! It had none of those swarms of beaters who frighten the game and toss them at your legs, stunned, pale with terror, nearly mincemeat. Three huntsmen for the packs, two whippers-in, and, of course, the hunting horn players – voilà, that was enough for twenty men! We would mount our horses at five o'clock, with Mass recited once to the dogs before they entered the forest undergrowth; at eight, we would track down the animal; at ten, we would lunch at Poitiers, as we allowed our horses to get their breath back; at night, at six, we would announce the kill within the walls of Vienna, Vienna in Austria, Messieurs!

"An archduke awaited us there. That is how the hunts once were! Yes, we were like that, and, at midnight, we waltzed at the empress's court ball – although by then our leather breeches were cooked. In our time, one did not wear a leather culotte more than once."

He mopped up his forehead with some tattered lace, for in his imagination Monsieur de Bougrelon had traveled so quickly from Poitiers, Poitou, to Vienna, Austria, that he was hot, the dear man, and fat drops of his makeup dribbled down his sweaty cheeks.

"He was a glamorous man," he went on, "with inexhaustible flair, and when I tell you what happened to him in Avranches with a certain Madame de Mertigny, a consummate dodo whose beauty was rather mature, you will love him as I do.

"Among other advantages (for he was as handsome as a Greek god), Monsieur de Mortimer had the smallest waist, a waist that was so supple and curved; and this opera girl's wasp waist earned him more than ten duels, as many with civilians as with officers of the guard, because his extravagant thinness – which was more than extravagant, it was unbelievable – rattled, disoriented, and enraged all the men, and, I will tell you, offended the women.

"Not all of them, but certainly those whom Mortimer was indifferent to, and Madame de Mertigny was one of these.

"Haughty and curt with his peers, Monsieur de Mortimer was lovably urbane with the humble; he was even familiar sometimes, but his familiarity was exquisite, as it seemed to beg people's pardon for dominating them and made those who served him adore him. Lauzun in the salons, but Duc de Beaufort in the servants' halls. Although he had a well-equipped house in Avranches, with a manservant, caterer, page, and groom, Monsieur de Mortimer was accustomed to having an old dressmaker, who had worked for his family for a long time, light his fires and bring up his hot water; she was a dreadful chaperone, half-blind, a little hunchbacked, and crippled too – terrible to look at, Messieurs – but she savagely adored the great madman Edgard.

"She had known him as a child . . . and he had the heart of a child, for he never aged.

"This mother Nidouille (the gnome in a skirt was grotesque down to her name) also lived in Avranches, on a pension that another Mortimer had left her. Edgard called her his *last* passion, and, in the morning, when the frightening Nidouille, her lips twitching, clomped into the room of that Homeric god, he would enjoy himself by asking her about the little events and opinions of the city from the depths of his great bed, and he would confess to the old servant the latest society scandals.

"One morning in January, to his ordinary question, 'Well, Madame Nidouille, what are they saying this morning in Avranches?' the old gorgon answered in her falsetto voice, 'They say, Monsieur de Mortimer, that you wear a corset.' Well, he suddenly straightened up and declared, 'Oh, they say I wear a corset! And who says that, Madame Nidouille?' 'Madame de Mertigny, from the corner of the square.' 'Ah! Madame de Mertigny claims I wear a corset! So you will tell her, Madame Nidouille, that it is being repaired, my corset. You will also tell her that with or without a corset, I, de Mortimer, Edgard, have a waistline that is ten centimeters smaller than hers, and I undertake to prove it . . . or rather, tell her nothing. Oh! This fussy female claims I wear a corset! I will burst hers or love is not my middle name.'

"And he did as he said. Although Mertigny was easily over thirty-five years old, and only as appealing as that, and though she was still prepared in *eau de lys* and had been battered by her hairdresser, Mortimer courted her, violated her rancid virtue, conquered her, and impregnated her. When the slanderer was quite pregnant – about to give birth, her waist spoiled, and keeping to her room for days at a time as she lay slumped on a sofa – Mortimer went to see her, his waist cinched under his Rhinegraves by one of the pretty woman's corsets (she had forgotten enough corsets at his house), and, after kissing her hand, asking about her, and caressing her lapdog, Mortimer suddenly rose, opening his Rhinegraves with a gesture. 'You said, Madame, that I wore a corset. Out of gallantry, I felt obliged to not make you a liar, and so I had to take yours, not knowing where to go. Do men know where these things are made? But see, Madame, to what extremes you made me go, forcing me to impregnate you to take it; you no longer wear corsets, and so, in your place, it is I who am encased! And won't you deign to remark that this woman's case does not embarrass me.' That was the man Mortimer was.

"How he loved the soul of Atala! The things he saw in it! His eloquence on the subject was remarkable and never ran dry. It was an eternally hot sea of glass, forests of madrepore corals and violet pendulums, with so many strange beings between its walls. 'Watch,' he would often tell me, his eyes fixed on the jar. 'The shadows of the great sailing ships are passing over the dahlias of the underwater forests; at this moment, I am in the shadows of whales who are going to the Pole! Right now, dockworkers are unloading ships heavy with snow at the port.' And he saw walruses and harbor seals swimming backward in the green cove water; those seals, long-haired as women and pink as girls, revealed themselves to him in the grottoes, and then he departed for Java, striding across terraces where the breeze from the open sea had a calm rhythm that swung the banana trees and flexible palms like so many fans; all the while, treacherous, racy images of the Asian countries, the golden cities of India, and the priestesses of Indra would pass before our eyes.

"We were forced to separate from the soul of Atala when Mortimer, ruined by the death of his uncle, de Blessemecourt, found himself suddenly without his income; eighty thousand *livres* a year slid between our fingers that day, and a whole drama unfolded, an unexpected, if not violent, death, an entire novel that I will recount to you one of these days, because now is the hour when I must go find the woman who would love to be another Barbara to me.

"We made the soul of Atala a gift to this lady. All the connoisseurs of Amsterdam gasped at our sale, there were bids that were truly mad, but we did not sell Atala – it would have been like selling a piece of our own soul. We saved a few jewels, keepsakes, miniatures, touching unwanted objects. You will see them at my home one night.

"The soul of Atala is at this woman's home. Conquered by our ideas, drunk with the glaucous, visionary charm that sleeps in preserving jars, this incomparable woman (I will take you to her) today possesses a museum, Messieurs, an impressive and well-done museum that will please you. But I must leave you: a woman does not wait."

CHAPTER TEN

THE TOWER OF WEEPING MEN

"A woman does not wait." That had been Monsieur de Bougrelon's farewell. We, on the other hand, waited for him in vain the next day and the two days that followed.

Monsieur de Bougrelon did not reappear; rain fell all the while, drowning the monotonous town in gray dampness until it was all mud and water; it was truly a country of ghosts, with Monsieur de Mortimer's heroic friend one of its unreal specimens, with his silhouette of a puppet, his jargon from another century, and his claims that were so many chimeras . . . Anyway, where could he be found? Monsieur de Bougrelon had utterly neglected to leave us his address – this was a typical habit of specters, which the illusory gentleman certainly had. Even his unexpected springing out of the shadows, his brusque disappearances . . . Having thought it over, we decided we had been dreaming. Our guide across Holland had abandoned us as soon as we had regained our composure. Monsieur de Bougrelon had been the product of our ennui, of an atmosphere of fog and a few bouts of *Schiedammer-*

induced drunkenness; we had given a body to our alcoholic reveries, a soul to the suggestions of museum paintings, a voice to the melancholies of the Prins Hendrikkade and the Noordzeekanaal; and, as it was under perpetual showers, the city, despite its radiant window displays and the dives of the Nes, from hour to hour became a city of spleen, and we decided to leave Amsterdam. Oh! Those three days of lost, gloomy wandering through special collections, those centuries of hours spent with eyes glued to magnifiers, scrutinizing unknown masters and showcases of jewels in the bland pepper-and-polish atmosphere of those amateurs' galleries.

The fourth morning, we had had enough. But the rain had broken, and the opaque fog that surrounded our windows was here and there becoming opalescent from a ray of sunshine. We closed our suitcases anyway, and, my fingers clenching a recalcitrant buckle, I was putting pressure on the abnormal bulge of my overnight bag with my knee when the door to my room opened wide, and with a formidable "Bonjour! Oh! You are leaving, Messieurs," his unexpected silhouette straightened in my doorway.

It was him: Monsieur de Bougrelon had returned to us. It was him, but this time even more fantastic and terrible, a Monsieur de Bougrelon that was sinister and macabre, because, on this last morning, a large black band cut his thin specter's face in two. Pale, his long dyed mustache spikier than ever, Monsieur de Bougrelon was wearing an eyepatch over one of his eyes; Monsieur de Bougrelon had come back to us one-eyed.

One hand on the turquoise head of an enormous cane, wearing a narrow olive redingote, Bougrelon arched his back and in a peremptory tone said, "I almost died, and but for the grace of God . . . Yes, Messieurs, a woman's gewgaw truly almost went into my eye, one of those gold needles that the little island women of Marken wear to decorate their foreheads like so many antennae . . . You know those little Salomes, they are the fishermen's delight here! My noble friend, the *dame de beauté* whom I play ombre with every night, hired one as a servant; since that delicate Gotte has a sweet, fresh little face, the other night, the night I left you actually, Messieurs (there are incomparable liqueurs in that house), I was descending the stairs (this girl preceded me, holding a torch), in a saucy mood – a ridiculous thing at my age, but after all, I am French – and grabbed the little thing by her waist, wanting to rub my old dog's snout in her peach skin. There were repercussions, Messieurs, because the surprised hen turned suddenly around and thrust her horn in my eye. In my eye, or very nearly! In the temple, it would have been instant death, Messieurs, and a just punishment for my bawdiness. To play Leandro[†] at my age! But thanks be to God, I am only a Horatius Cocles, and that better suits my beauty; admit it, Messieurs. Inês de Castro was one-eyed and a king of Spain loved her. So I am from the House of Castro and that consoles me, because, although Norman, I am also from Toledo through a foremother – from Castro, not castrated! Ha ha! Don't get mixed up.

[†] A stock character of the Italian *commedia dell'arte*; one of the Lovers (*Innamorati*).

"But I am right on time: you are leaving, and I can shake your hand. You are taking the eleven o'clock train – twenty minutes later, and I would have missed you. I would not have forgiven myself, Messieurs, because, thanks to you, by helping you see the city, I relived the Amsterdam of Monsieur de Mortimer. Frenchmen like you are a rare godsend in the dreary era that I still linger in. One sees nothing here but flea-market princes and traveling salesmen. You must have thought I was dead and I should have told you, I know, but a person bores his friends with these little trifles . . . Ah! You are leaving: the fog of this country is poisoning you – only an exile can like Amsterdam. You are leaving and maybe we will never see each other again." Pulling a huge leather chronometer from his fob pocket, a sort of navigator's compass-watch, he said, "Ten to eleven. You missed your train, Messieurs, and thanks to me. Yes, I am proud of that and applaud myself; it was hard for me to see you leave without having knocked back a few *Schiedammers* together. You will not deny me the honor of having you at my table today. I invite you to lunch – I will treat this time."

And that morning we dined again with Monsieur de Bougrelon. Following his commendable habit, he left it to us to settle the bill, but he had lost his customary loquacity and good humor; a visible anxiety troubled the indefatigable talker. Was it the malaise inherent in every departure? It was as though something was broken between us; an atmosphere of sadness and mistrust filled the vaulted little underground room of the Staawertstraat restaurant. And then, too, his recent accident might have been bothering the old gentleman, because twice Monsieur de Bougrelon rose to go to the kitchen and refresh his compresses and moisten his eye; Gotte's gold pin was evidently still making him suffer.

"In Avranches, back when Monsieur de Mortimer and I were making women miserable, this scratch would have healed in an hour. In an hour – what am I saying? In five minutes the skin would have been stitched, bandaged, and the flesh as smooth as fruit . . . Monsieur de Mortimer had a marvelous ointment, Messieurs. I have sadly lost the formula. The formula dated from the Crusades, Messieurs, a prince of the House of Bouillon, who has since died in the Holy Land, brought it from the Orient, from Jerusalem, or rather Persepolis, and Mortimer's family received it from a princess of Clèves who was allied with or descended from those very Bouillons. It included a thousand different ingredients, hyssop, bat's hair, antimony, crushed emeralds, and essence of mummy, Messieurs, a veritable Egyptian pharmacopoeia – but that doesn't matter. Edgard used it frequently, whatever it was, and to miraculous effect. I will give you this example:

"Every morning when we were in Avranches, Monsieur de Mortimer would go down to the kennels and later the stables to stroke the animals (he was mad about horses and dogs) and, if necessary, to correct the grooms and whippers-in; like a big child, he would throw whole loaves of bread to the mastiff packs, offer watermelon slices to the stallions, pat the mares' chests, pinch the fillies' noses, and let lumps of sugar be eaten out of his hand.

"Well, on one of his rounds of the stables, Mortimer tickled a large Hungarian horse as he passed, which Edgard thought was a gelding, but which was as whole as you or I, Messieurs, and this great chestnut nag lashed out at Mortimer and bit him cruelly . . . He bit him on his face, Messieurs, just like an apple. It was a hideous injury, an abominable injury: the whole jaw was cut away, a gaping wound that dashed the heroic beauty of the admirable cavalier forever.

"Another man would have killed the beast. A horse falls from a pistol shot just like a man . . . Mortimer, though, went up to his room, took out a jar of his ointment, rubbed it on his cheek . . . and that evening he dined in the city . . . for by that evening the wound had disappeared.

"That is how they were, Messieurs – the ointments and the men of our epoch. Compare them, if you dare, to the inventions of your time."

That was the only bit of bragging where Monsieur de Bougrelon's ordinarily sparkling, now subdued fantasies rose up during our gloomy lunch. He did not pick up his bombastic speech and haughty diction again until we reached the Prins Hendrikkade, almost at the edge of the IJ,[†] and were in front of the Schreierstoren, which he was anxious to show us that day.

When we had arrived before this great mass of stone, he said, "The *Tower of Weeping Men*, Messieurs. In France it would have been called the Tower of Weeping *Women*, because men do not know tears in France, or at least they are not supposed

† Amsterdam's waterfront; an inland arm of the IJsselmeer in the Netherlands.

to. Sorrow is essentially feminine, but these good Dutch do not have such foresight. Joris, Jan, or Peter left for Borneo, Sumatra, Java, or America; Peter's father, Jan's brother, and Joris's grandfather accompanied them to the boat and there, on the quay, squeezed them in their big arms, with big tears in these big men's big eyes – seals' tears and porpoises' sobs, tears that hardly beautified their china-blue eyes, for all the old ugly creatures of Delft, as Teniers and all the Van Ostades and Sans Ostades of this country of wind and windmills painted; and so it is with farewells, remorse, and despair that the stones of this tower were cemented, Messieurs. The French tradition, which is a tradition of noblewomen, would have made women in love cry here; the Dutch, who are realists, made one sob over old sorrows, the *Tower of Weeping Men.*

"Today I too want to cry, mostly for myself and a little for you, Messieurs. This is where my vanity tells me to say goodbye.

"We will not see each other again: people do not come back to Holland. The dreams people take away from this place, the memories of it, are more beautiful than the reality; one must never go back. Me, I am an outcast, an old madman cloistered in a vision that I do not want to touch. I am an urn, Messieurs, but an urn that is still warm from the heat of the embers. These embers are visions of my past, visions of France as I knew it – as I left it – a France without railroads, without telegraphs, without telephones, a France not yet disgraced by factories and parliaments. In this country of canals, at least I will see neither bicycles nor automobiles, a thousand hideous and barbaric things that I cannot even imagine because I close my eyes to them, but whose names alone make me suffer. And Monsieur de Mortimer, or his ghost, still fills this city. He is beside me when I walk along these canals; he speaks quietly to me as I slowly roam around, at night, at twilight, in our dear museum. The portraits that we once loved together smile at me, gesture to me, look at me with our former bond. For me, Amsterdam is crowded with my cherished phantoms, Messieurs. That is why I want to die here."

CHAPTER ELEVEN

DAME DE BEAUTÉ

"No, Messieurs, I will never see France again," Monsieur de Bougrelon sadly chanted.

He had crossed his arms over his chest, and his gaze had become strangely distant.

"Anyway, what would I do there? Everyone I loved there is dead, I no longer know anyone, and – what is even worse – no one knows me there anymore either.

"An exile is always alone, but perhaps less so in the land of his exile than in his own country. One must never be tempted by the joys of return; think what it would be like after thirty or forty years away! If one finds only an empty house, that is not half bad. Ghosts have a strange preference for old houses – and how many sleeping memories they hold, how many deathly dormant swallows, wings outstretched, can be found between the ceiling beams! That would be my dream, to go back to an empty house and an abandoned garden, but one never has the chance to return and knock on a rusty gate and closed louvered shutters. No, the gate is newly painted, the shutters open, the garden kept, the paths raked, and geraniums are blooming in the flower beds, Messieurs! Geraniums . . . where one left columbines, blue aconites, and exquisitely graceful, old-fashioned hollyhocks; and in the house, there are strangers . . . strangers! Feel how insulting that word is, Messieurs! Faces that you do not know, which stare at you, mistrustful faces, hostile faces, the vile, bourgeois features of landowners!

"The house belongs to me; you're the one to leave it.[†]

"No, I will not expose myself to that horrible welcome, to that knife blow to my old heart! At least here, so distant and removed, I see the old mansion where I grew up in Avranches exactly as I left it; and it is my Childhood and my dear Past, when I was twenty-five years old, that, in my thoughts, appear to me forever crouching, the two of them, by the fireplace, my Childhood like an old servant, a trembling octogenarian grandmother, and my Past still young and handsome as though it were fifty years ago, half a century, Messieurs! For only our childhood ages in our memories, while our youth is protected by love; the age in which one loved blazes like an intense sunrise . . . but my two dear ghosts have not awaited me. A long time ago the Bougrelon home was put up for sale. Twenty years ago it was the town's general revenue office; pencil pushers, bureaucrats with ink on their asses, moved in there. Perhaps it is a rotisserie today . . . Can you see me disembarking, Messieurs, to find my treasured specters there,

---

[†] *"La maison est à moi, c'est à vous d'en sortir."* Derived from Molière's *Tartuffe*.

turning a spit or serving meals? ... Did I not tell you? I have lived in Holland for more than thirty years of my exile's life. I must die, and I want to die here."

Monsieur de Bougrelon did not have his habitual grandiloquence anymore, and his theatrical gestures were gone. He spoke with his back arched, but his shoulders less thrown back, and his two hands rested on the head of his cane; his intent eagle's eye, cloudy now, astonished us with its softness. Monsieur de Bougrelon almost spoke like other men. He was an unknown Bougrelon – a man had emerged from the puppet. In that corseted being, made up and stiff in his studied posture, there was, after all, humility, true sorrow, and pain.

The bleak and sandy stretch of water that was the Zuiderzee was before us, with shifting foam cresting on the horizon (for the sea wind had begun to rise) and russet clouds that would suddenly tear open to show scraps of blue atmosphere; these clouds swept the sky, the truly Dutch sky of painters, evoking windmill blades, lighthouse beacons, and fishing-boat yards, with, very far away on our right, the enormous round mass of the Tower of Weeping Men.

Monsieur de Bougrelon had become quiet, and, since his heart was heavy with the melancholy of our goodbyes, we respected his silence.

We strode this way for nearly ten minutes along the banks, down the Prins Hendrikkade.

"But I do not want to keep you, Messieurs," our guide brusquely interrupted. "I already made you miss your train this morning, and once is enough. Leave, yes, it is time. I've started to like you, Messieurs, and tomorrow I would suffer too much to see you go. The heart of an old man is like ivy. A person gets attached quickly when he is alone."

But he corrected himself almost immediately:

"Alone! No, I am not alone. Because I did not have the strongest ties keeping me here, divine grace placed near me a devoted and attentive beauty who would like to be another Barbara for me; she provides the most noble and delicate affection for my exile and old age, this *dame de beauté* whose admirable collection I promised to show you one day! Her collection of preserves, the preserves! One of the unexpected relics of this country of visionaries.

"Yes, I remember now, I made you a promise, and I would have taken you there, but then we went about our other activities. We do what we wish, eh? And anyway, I was too excited when I described those preserving jars. The visit would have perhaps disappointed you, and I would not have forgiven your disappointment, I admit that. You lent your souls to my ramblings, to the reveries of this old madman, and I am infinitely grateful, Messieurs, that you let me cultivate the fantasies of my dreams through you . . . It is like the little house I live in; I should have welcomed you inside. A pied-à-terre, really, a little roost for a former *demi-solde,* but I have a few curious knickknacks there that are priceless to me: a miniature of Barbara, the one of Mércèdes with its frame of rubies, and a few gems, castoffs from a happier age. I should have shown you all of this. But we ran out of time, and I was carried away by the wind of other caprices – besides, those trinkets are only valuable to the one who owns them.

"A portrait is always a betrayal; the only ones worth it are those of strangers. And anyway, what would you have thought of me after visiting my rathole? . . . A rathole, yes, Messieurs, it would be a rathole in France, but thanks to the meticulous Dutch cleanliness, it is an attic room here. What would you have thought, seeing a Bougrelon live like this? I am poor, what can you do! No, you would have thought nothing, because I know how delicate your souls are; better, you will never think or believe anything disagreeable about me, Messieurs, even if one day someone tells you a bit of mean gossip about the name of Bougrelon. That, I know."

He abruptly put his cane beneath his arm to take our hands, and while he held them tenderly in his own hands: "This rathole of a fallen gentleman, this monk's cell, Messieurs, I would have taken you to regardless, if I had had a portrait of Mortimer there to show you.

"My friend de Mortimer! I have told you so much about him that you almost know him, and I would have liked to etch the indelible traits of his heroic and charming face in your memory, but alas I do not even have the shape. I had more than ten portraits of Edgard, and I burned them all – none of them resembled him.

"Farewell, Messieurs." And with an unexpected pirouette, he turned on his heels and disappeared, looking as though he had just fallen into the canal.

We thought we would never see Monsieur de Bougrelon again.

A mysterious person, he took with him the enigma of his life, leaving us with an astounding obsession.

The story would have been perfectly harmonious had it ended there; unfortunately, perfect harmony exists only in adventures that one invents, and Monsieur de Bougrelon is not an invented character.

We saw him that very night, and in the most fortuitous, the most unexpected, the most ordinary circumstances.

Chance – which brought his hallucinatory silhouette out of the shadows for us – snatched the mask from the phantom on the very night of our solemn goodbyes, bringing down the scaffolding that he had so laboriously raised with his many heroic claims.

It was preordained that we would miss our train twice that day. Returning to the hotel, we ran into a friend from Paris who had arrived at noon, while we were lunching in the city, and who had waited resolutely for us by the *Adrian*. He had learned we were in Amsterdam from a glance at the passenger list, and the dear Pointel, delighted with his stroke of good luck, did not intend to release us.

"A pure accident, but one that benefits me," he declared as he seized us in the lobby, "I am not letting you go. It is my first time in Amsterdam, you've been here for eight days, you're clued-in and you've done your reading on the best museums and walks, and I will let you go? No! I'm not that foolish."

As we objected (our packed bags, our return tickets): "Bah!

You will give me tonight. You have plenty of time to guide me until midnight. It's done, we will eat together. I am inviting you, and you will show me all the splendors of the Nes tonight. I was just nosing around there, and the twilight was so strange that a hunter couldn't tell a dog from a wolf."

"Depraved, of course!"

We could not refuse to steer a compatriot in distress around Amsterdam's legendary Venusberg, and it would only be for one night after all. So we accepted Pointel's invitation; after finishing our coffees, we led him to the Nes.

Yet we did not go to the Nes, but rather to the Zeedijk, that neighborhood of sailors and shady bars, a little like old Marseille's port neighborhood and the former Rietdijk of Antwerp, a distant suburb behind the lonely station reserved for the frolicking of the cosmopolitan navy and the basest prostitutes.

The place is quite dangerous; sailors' drunkenness, aggravated by lust, easily leads to knife fights, and the canal is so useful for pesky corpses in foggy Holland! The Zeedijk is a neighborhood of cabarets, dances, *cafés-concerts*; people love with their every gesture and sing in every language. In the Zeedijk you find the great Dutch criminal underworld dancing, hollering, fornicating.

We were together, and, fortified by a translator, we bravely entered the Zeedijk.

We had already visited five or six dives in the area when, in a cabaret where sailors danced, a place that was both a bar and a ballroom, in the thick, reddish-brown air typical of these kinds of places, steaming with breath, smoky with tobacco, smelling of acrid sweat and alcohol, stinking sharply of tar, where everything floated in one of those oily gleams of light so dear to Rembrandt's brush, what did we see?

Sitting on the stage reserved for the orchestra, towering with his bow over the kinky heads of Negro sailors and the caps of American seamen who were dancing a joyful polka, what did we see? Ghostly and stiff, his olive redingote pinching his waist and a black eyepatch over his eye: Monsieur de Bougrelon!

Calm and pale, his chin resting on a violin, Monsieur de Bougrelon was making the clientele dance in their sailors' smocks and dance-hall boots. Around him were crowds of polka dancers, awkwardly turning two by two, their hands on each other's shoulders, jumping and laughing.

Monsieur de Bougrelon, with his profile of an old wounded eagle beneath his black eyepatch, was taller than all of them and loomed like a statue of Orpheus, but a macabre Orpheus, accompanied by a withered and pitiful Eurydice in tartan; for there was an elderly harpist sitting next to Monsieur de Bougrelon, a lamentable carcass of a grandmother in an immense Pamela hat, with a faded old checkered shawl draped over her shabby dress of formerly green silk. An antique Empire harp cried sadly beneath her hands, which were clad in fingerless gloves, while Monsieur de Bougrelon's hand – a hand that was all skin and bones – convulsed like a crab along his violin, restless and frenetic fingers contracting and flying. And we realized where the old gentleman spent his evenings.

We possessed the key to the mystery; we knew why our dear old guide left us so suddenly every night; we understood, and with what sadness, the kind of game of ombre (and not of *ombres,* shadows, but of ghosts, he should have said) that the old gentleman played with the noblewoman who wanted the best for him.

What! This was the *dame de beauté,* the woman with the private chapel where he listened, every Sunday . . . and what about Mass and Vespers . . . the woman with the museum of preserves, the other Barbara, etc.! Monsieur de Bougrelon had brazenly lied, and Monsieur de Mortimer, and their heroic and magnificent youth, and the duels, the adventures, and his exile, the eyepatch over his eye . . . in similar circles, some scuffle surely . . . or some blow received in a scrap . . .

Monsieur de Bougrelon was a musician at a sailors' bar.

We remained, stupefied, in the entrance to the dance hall . . .

Monsieur de Bougrelon raised his head and saw us.

Not a muscle moved in his pale face, and, tragically, he continued to play as though nothing had happened. Lowering his eyelid, he shut the only eye he had left.

Monsieur de Bougrelon did not want to see us.

Respecting his wishes, we left without acknowledging him.

EPILOGUE

He appeared to me. He, yes, He, who had enchanted and now made me regret my short stay in the land of canals and windmills, He with the ghostly silhouette, the illustrious speech, the epic grandiloquence that had animated and populated the mists of Amsterdam and the North Sea, the man whose châteaux in Spain he evoked with one word, with one gesture, but with what a brilliant word and what a superb gesture, in the fog and drizzle of Holland!

The man who brought to life the portraits at the museum and the gallant castoffs of bygone centuries, and who made jars of preserves speak directly to our souls, yes, the magician of Zeedijk, of old frames and glass cases, Monsieur de Bougrelon revealed himself to me after only a year in the middle of Provence – a Provence that was rainy and bleak, a sunless Provence decomposing beneath showers that made it sadder than the sandy dunes of the unhappy Netherlands – and in rather unique circumstances.

There were three manifestations.

The first one took place in Marseille, which was still dripping wet from the downpour of January 1, 1898, but had already warmed up thanks to two mornings of beautiful sunshine.

It was Monday, the third of that month, around noon actually, at the hour when La Canebière is swarming and crawling with the incessant comings and goings of its cosmopolitan crowds, who walk up and down the famous Allées by the Vieux-Port shipyards. On the Quai de la Fraternité, there were the regular gatherings of dockhands and thugs savoring clams and sea urchins at the shellfish merchants' stalls, side by side with the big traders of the city! For it was also the hour when the Bourse is in full swing . . . In the sunny warmth of Roi René's celestial fireplace, between Place Victor-Gelu and the Église des Augustins,[†] returning from La Joliette, dockworkers and port caulkers were having fun, chatting and playful . . .

Oh! Those smells of garlic and bouillabaisse!

Intoxicated by the crowd, whose anonymity enchanted me, I mixed with the people and let myself be swept into a circle of onlookers around a kiosk.

A group was moving around there, of shoeshine boys and fishwives, even working girls from La Tourette flirting with tobacco chewers, and all of them jeering with shiny eyes and black pupils, thick lips pulled back over white teeth, this whole

---

[†] French, *l'église de Saint-Augustin.* Likely a reference to Église Saint-Ferréol-les-Augustins, located at the old port of Marseille.

little world curiously leaning over two pitiful burnooses that had wound up on the ground, two old Arabs in hoods, a heap of lousy rags and exhausted flesh, fallen there out of weariness, right beneath the strollers' feet.

With two long waxen faces, long white beards, and extinguished pupils, the two Arabs had faces of ancient prophets and remained still beneath the people's inquisitive eyes, indifferent, as though far away in the parvis of their mosque, while their mummies' hands continued to involuntarily knead the wrinkled yellow soles of their naked feet. Surely two passengers who had disembarked that very morning – on Mondays transport ships arrive from Tunis and Algiers.

In front of them were the masts of the Vieux-Port and the blue of the deceitful sea. With their profiles of old camels, oh how they smelled of the plague and the Orient, of bazaar spices and palm wine, those two pitiable wrecks from Algeria, collapsed on the ground of their exile!

"From Mecca to *m . . . de*!"[†]

And the blaring voice, which summarized the situation so well in a few words, risked the last one out of nowhere . . . So insulting was his barb for the port of Marseille, and so powerfully and unexpectedly did he define those two poor Orientals' exodus, that I could not contain a smile. I turned around to wink at the author of the bold remark. But there was no one there but the people of Marseille; I had imagined it, unless I had thought out loud.

"From Mecca to *m . . . de*!" That was not my language, so

† *Merde* (shit).

where had I heard that imperious voice, that emphatic timbre, those stressed syllables ... ?

Only Monsieur de Bougrelon would have had the audacity to make the comparison, that surprise within the ellipsis, only he, with the voice of a *maréchal de camp* opening fire; but I confess, to my shame, that I did not consider it for a minute, and without spending more time on pointless reflections, I returned to pack my bags at the hotel, because I was leaving that very night for Toulon.

Toulon, its placid harbor, blue as silk beneath a hot sun, at the foot of scorching mountains; the back and forth of its boatmen, chatting barefoot on the Quai de la Vieille Darse as white awnings flap; its open cirque within wooded hills; Saint-Mandrier and Tamaris; and between the high silhouettes of its fanciful battleship factories, the flash and dash of the officers' boats and the double streams of oars sparkling with water and sunlight – Toulon in May, Toulon in June, Toulon of summer, Toulon of joy, Toulon of passionate Mocotie[†] and jubilant Provence, which I never should have rediscovered!

Cities of the Midi, whose charm is their light, and whose beauty is their mirage, we must never see you in winter! No, Toulon is not gay beneath the rain! The mountains are hard and gray upon a sky of haze, and in the damp shadows and muddy stinking streets, the Provence woman's amber coloring and skin tone become dubiously pale, and all the strapping

[†] An obsolete term for the region of Provence. Similarly, *moco* (masculine) and *mocote* (feminine) denote inhabitants of Provence, and more specifically, sailors from Toulon and Marseille.

and aloof *moco* guys, ruddy and healthy in their threadbare, disheveled summer clothes, become so pitiful bundled up in winter wools, their complexions grimy and their gestures clumsy in the fisherman's smocks and knitted cardigans of the northern worker . . .

Walking beneath the leafless plane trees that lined the paths, I was sorry to not find the luminous piles of yellow carnations that fill the markets in June; or the tender sprays of pink carnations, which smell so delicately of vanilla; or the moist skin of beautiful red carnations, those flashy things (oh! the poor little anemic roses and ill-timed mimosas of the so-called Nice flower shipments!), and so beneath the pounding rain I went back up the Port Marchand walkway. There, before the cloudy horizon, I remembered the turquoise dusk of green and pink gold of that past summer night when, amidst odors of sweat and tar, of cold cream and oranges, I picked up some delicious jargon from the mouth of a Toulon girl in a floral percale shift. The pretty girl! Surely she was a *mocote* from a long line of fishermen, for she was a well-built brunette, her beauty soft and unrefined. Her two hands resting on a seaman's shoulder, the amorous *mocote* warbled these words:

"Let's go into the pine forest – it will be a cooler place for us to fool around. But don't open your eyes so big, you'll frighten me."

A wild flight of oilskin sailor's coats in the darkness, a hoarse call of the distant tram going toward Mourillon, and two swabbies splashing around in puddles of mud, their backs rounded beneath the same umbrella – that is a Toulon twilight in winter.

And the same voice that spoke to me in Marseille chanted these words in my ear: "Coming back – how reckless!"

When I turned around, I saw no more than I did before, back on the quay of the old port.

A shadow was watching over me; an invisible presence accompanied me; an awful wisdom spoke for me.

With the taste for debauchery that brings us sadness and ennui, I slowly approached the mean streets of the famous Chapeau-Rouge quarter, where the Toulon aediles claim to confine prostitution – yes, the Chapeau-Rouge, which is as renowned in the annals of the navy as the Coin de Reboul in Marseille and the former Rietdijk of Antwerp.

In the middle of a stream of berets and sailor's coats, the Cristal-Bar had once sparkled in the glare of dazzling lights. All mirrors and marble, it was a great room fully open to the street, and so luxurious it put to shame the percale house-coats and Turkey-red robes the girls wore in the houses across the road.

We danced in this bar; an old orchestrion, cranked by a cheerful sailor, produced tired waltzes and polkas, while middies and swabbies in immense blue collars of the state and white marine infantry helmets jostled, whirled, and pranced pell-mell with the *mocos* and boatmen of the port.

Men reigned here, because the Cristal-Bar was forbidden to women; a girl introduced into so much virility, with all the inevitable risks, would have burst. Under the friendly eye of the police, they all waltzed there – Marius and my brother Yves,[†] all the friendships of the navy watch, Baptistin and Tann, all the tropical encounters – with hands on shoulders, suddenly serious, eyes lowered and teeth clenched, in the physical pleasure of the dance, jealously observed from across the street by the women's blackened eyes.

Now I found the Chapeau-Rouge, in keeping with the city, soul-sucking and bleak, a wintry Chapeau-Rouge, its alleys almost deserted; here and there was the silhouette of a swabbie who had washed up in a dive bar, a sad girl sitting on the table in front of him, pouring him a drink; no more cursing, no more joyful hoots; in the dubious cul-de-sacs, muddy espadrilles fled with catlike stealth, men who looked like pimps had hushed conversations, and, finally, in the middle of the street, there was a black patch, blacker than night, of shutters closed over the entire façade of the Cristal-Bar, and on a paper posted on the door, these simple words: *"Closed due to change of ownership."*

Closed! The Cristal-Bar was closed! Why had I come back?

A hooded figure leaned against the front window – I did not notice him at first – a sort of man covered up to the eyes in a long black reefer jacket, who took a step toward me and said in a voice that I had heard before:

"To have had the happiness of loving a place, and there to have known the joy of living and letting live; to have had such vertigo from a feeling that you could pass your shivers to

[†] Possibly a reference to Pierre Loti's 1883 novel *Mon Frère Yves*, about a friendship at sea between an educated officer and a semi-literate, hard-drinking sailor.

others, and then to dare to return, to hope to revive the dead without thinking for a minute that the irrevocable hour turns everything that we love into dust and nothingness, that the past is a mass grave, and that, outside of our heart, everything down here is a sepulcher!"

Like all specters, the man did not have a face, and yet I recognized him! It was Him! Only he, the poor musician of sailors' dives in Amsterdam, could have conjured himself in the doorway of this dance hall for marine squadrons.

"But a memory, Monsieur . . . A person can cloister himself in a memory, he can wall himself away in bygone happiness like a monk immured in a cell! But, Monsieur, when you have one, a memory is to be respected, and the memory that you had, you, of this region, what a luminous prison for a soul! What use was my example to you – I who never wanted to return to France out of fear that I would not rediscover what I had left there, I who for thirty years of my life roamed in exile in the company of a ghost? . . . You should have died in Toulon, Monsieur – never left or else never come back . . . If I had left Amsterdam for a single day, do you think that I would have found Monsieur de Mortimer in Amsterdam again?"

The man without a face had vanished. I shivered, thinking about the soul that had spoken to me . . . at a year's distance, from Holland to Provence, from Amsterdam to Toulon.

A shadow's mouth had uttered my thoughts out loud.

And I knew that Monsieur de Bougrelon was dead.

AFTERWORD BY THE TRANSLATOR

"That is how they were, Messieurs – the ointments and the men of our epoch. Compare them, if you dare, to the inventions of your time." Thus declares Amsterdam's forgotten puppet Monsieur de Bougrelon in this astonishing, hallucinatory novella.

To compare *Monsieur de Bougrelon* – which was published serially in *Le Journal* from January 30 to May 10, 1897 – to the novels of our time is to be thrust into the same wonderful nostalgia as Lorrain's characters feel. The novella's inventiveness and sheer Decadence find kindred spirits in the works of Comte de Lautréamont, Joris-Karl Huysmans, and even Louis-Ferdinand Céline, but not in the spare, personal novellas and overblown tomes of today. *Monsieur de Bougrelon*'s deranged characters; its indulgent language, which varies from obscure to invented to slang; and its unconventional vision of art and sex make a person long for the *fin de siècle*. Things were not simpler then, but they were more amusing.

Thankfully these Decadent works live on – some are forgotten, some remembered: literary *Boudoirs of the Dead,* as Monsieur de Bougrelon would say, luminous prisons for the soul.

Jean Lorrain and his literary output have largely been forgotten. There are certainly many reasons for this, but one must be Lorrain's personality.

"An extravagant dandy, avowed ether addict, known homosexual, and hopeless gossip, Jean Lorrain provoked every emotion in his contemporaries – except one: indifference" (Phillip Winn, translated from *Sexualités décadentes chez Jean Lorrain*). He provoked his fellow writers with his scathing columns, which made him as popular as Truman Capote when he was publishing excerpts from *Answered Prayers* – to the horror of New York City's socialites. Lorrain also frightened some with his satanism, and others with his homosexuality, and still others with his rampant use of the drug ether. He scandalized the aristocrats of the South of France and lampooned them in his novels.

A friend, the author Edmond de Goncourt, wondered, "What's Lorrain's dominant trait? Is it spite or a complete lack of tact?"

Lorrain led a life that shed its conventional upper-middle-class Norman upbringing to embrace the principles of Decadence and dandyism. He briefly lived in a Parisian apartment that he decorated with such lack of restraint, as befitting only Joris-Karl Huysmans' Duc des Esseintes, that it promptly gave him nightmares and he had to move out. In fact, Jean Lorrain was close friends with *À rebours* author Huysmans; however, when Lorrain was charged with corrupting public morals by literary means – the same charge leveled at Charles Baudelaire's *Les Fleurs du mal* – Huysmans did not come to his defense.

In true nineteenth-century fashion, both Guy de Maupassant and Paul Verlaine challenged Lorrain to a duel. At last, Lorrain had his duel: after writing some characteristically harsh words and insinuations about Marcel Proust's *Les Plaisirs et les Jours,* Lorrain found himself twenty-fives paces away from the duel-happy Proust. Both authors shot their pistols; both left the forest unscathed.

Here is the French author Léon Daudet on Jean Lorrain: "Lorrain had the big chubby face of a vicious hairdresser, with his hair parted and smelling of patchouli, his bulging eyes – astonished and hungry – and thick lips that salivated, spat, and splashed as he spoke [. . .] He greedily nourished himself on all manner of slander and filth." In an interview in Nice, Lorrain remarked, "What helps me live is knowing that so many people find me odious."

By all accounts, Lorrain was as over the top as his character Monsieur de Bougrelon. He wore a carnation in his buttonhole and plenty of makeup, and one photograph even shows him dressed as a Celtic warrior at Sarah Bernhardt's home in 1895. He was also too shocking, and too gay, for the France he lived in. His reputation began to supersede his literary accomplishments, until both his accomplishments and his reputation eroded into the country's collective memory. Neither Jean Lorrain nor *Monsieur de Bougrelon,* however, deserves this modern amnesia.

In 1896, Jean Lorrain visited Holland with his friend, the writer and bibliophile Octave Uzanne (1851–1931). This trip must have been a disappointment, for *Monsieur de Bougrelon* is a book about creativity, which is to say it is a book about boredom. Not just boredom, of course, but *ennui* – its cultivation is a dandy's true métier. And so this novella begins where most others end: a couple of French tourists have seen all the sights, from the lofty museums to the bawdy red-light districts to the vibrant street scenes of Amsterdam; these sights delighted them; and now they are bored. Hopelessly bored.

At this point Monsieur de Bougrelon makes his spectral entrance, and he revives the city of Amsterdam for the complacent Frenchmen by speaking, by naming objects, by turning Amsterdam into a city of Decadent memories and dreams. Monsieur de Bougrelon, in turn, takes his inspiration from the even-more-spectral and remote Monsieur de Mortimer. The memories – or rather, the fantasies – that Monsieur de Bougrelon has of Monsieur de Mortimer make life in Amsterdam bearable. Indeed, life for everyone in this novella (other than the prosaic, simple Dutch) is a vertiginous pit of ennui that only the fantasy of memory and the Decadent imagination can relieve.

One form of relief from the bland nausea of everyday life is through imaginary pleasures, or *hypothétiques luxures*. Imaginary pleasures are the transfigurations of people, animals, and objects into loci of intense sexual attraction or obsession. The ability to do that, Jean Lorrain's work seems to say, lies at the heart of the Decadent imagination. Decadence is not about things that are just *so* refined, *so* tasteful, but about cultivating a state of mind that will allow an intelligent person to live through this modern age of tedium without committing suicide.

After all, what could be less typically "Decadent" than a jar of dreary Dutch asparagus? Not much, one would think, but with the extravagant guide of Monsieur de Bougrelon, these jars are transformed into glaucous, museum-worthy phalluses, simply by virtue of their ability to encapsulate the past.

It is surrealist before there was surrealism. The character of Boorluut – inspired by Georges Rodenbach's Joris Borluut in *Le Carillonneur* (1897) – presents a model case: this mysterious Belgian fell in love with the bells of Bruges' belfry and loved them "like they were girls, like working girls, Messieurs, and took the same sensual and carnal delight in swinging them that you or I take in screwing tarts." For the characters who are gripped by such an imaginary pleasure, there is nothing more serious than their new objects of desire, no matter how incongruous they seem. These transformations are grotesquely hilarious; their recitations invite a special type of laughter, half-horrified and half-incredulous.

One example among many: Monsieur de Bougrelon – after describing his obsession with a chaste woman named

Barbara van Mierris, and describing her brutal murder, and insinuating that she had sex with her ornately dressed female monkey, and suggesting that her Ethiopian servant-slave murdered her out of jealousy of the animal – pulls out a beautiful, unique pocket mirror and remarks, "It came from Barbara, Messieurs. It was her guenon's mirror."

On nearly every page of *Monsieur de Bougrelon* there is just such an absurd connection, a similar transformation of the prosaic into the sublime and back again. Though only the tale of the guenon's mirror provokes the narrator's "crazed laughter," this laughter permeates the book, ready to erupt, as the ordinary narrator encounters grotesque metamorphoses. The story of Barbara van Mierris itself does not end there: its denouement occurs when the aristocratic and normally blasé Monsieur de Mortimer murders a street poodle – provoking the bemused realization, "We were dealing with a madman," spoken through the narrator's undoubtedly gritted teeth.

To go through life, to travel, to experience new and old things while trying to avoid such imaginary pleasures would be asinine ("and worse, impotent"). Even the narrator and his unnamed French friend experience such a transformation as they stand in front of a Kalverstraat shop window, admiring Dutch furs and leathers that come alive for them. And the character of Monsieur de Bougrelon, the narrator wonders in a sober moment – could he have been "the product of our ennui, of an atmosphere of fog and a few bouts of *Schiedammer*-induced drunkenness"? A grotesquely hilarious imaginary pleasure, in other words?

Whether "real" or not, Monsieur de Bougrelon leaves nothing behind for the narrator to obsess over, or wear, or hang on his walls.

There is a fascinating distinction in the way that desirable men and women are described in *Monsieur de Bougrelon*. The desirable women, including Barbara van Mierris, are neurotically chaste and typically meet tragic ends; at which point, Monsieur de Bougrelon and Monsieur de Mortimer's attraction transfers to *something* else. After the Spanish Marquise dies, Monsieur de Bougrelon obsesses over her rubies, now in a rosary above her miniature portrait. When the canine Barbara dies, Monsieur de Bougrelon wears her fur as a muff. Even Monsieur de Bougrelon's interest in his *dame de beauté* is transformed into a much more psychotic fascination with her museum of preserves.

This is not the case, however, for the male characters. Monsieur de Mortimer, for example, is the ultimate object of desire – he is certainly more desirable than any of the freakish noblewomen and prostitutes that the novella catalogs – and, pointedly, Monsieur de Bougrelon tells his French companions that he burned all of Monsieur de Mortimer's portraits because none resembled him. Even Monsieur de Mortimer's wound-healing potion is lost. Compared to the women, who are immortalized in portraits and various objects, Monsieur de Mortimer is unique.

Monsieur de Mortimer may be a figment of Monsieur de Bougrelon's addled mind, just as Monsieur de Bougrelon may be a figment of the narrator's imagination; yet, nevertheless, the two fantastical aristocrats do have a real relationship, and some of the most compelling speeches revolve around Monsieur de Bougrelon's feelings toward Monsieur de Mortimer. There is love between them, one that exceeds mere "loyalty," one that cannot be transfigured into anything else.

Jean Lorrain's perspective as a gay man sets this novel apart from many others of its time. It far preceded the works of Jean Genet and Jean Cocteau. Marcel Proust's *Sodome and Gomorrhe* came out twenty-four years after *Monsieur de Bougrelon*, and even then it was critically reviled. In the 1920s, when André Gide defended homosexuality, he was also condemned. And so the latent homosexuality of *Monsieur de Bougrelon* got the silent treatment from some critics:

> [Monsieur de Bougrelon] knows no one, but he speaks mysteriously if respectfully of an old lady, a beautiful old lady, whom he visits every night. Together they discuss the old world and the new world; together they forget their loneliness, their decline. M. de Bougrelon takes his leave at the same hour every evening, explaining that the beautiful old lady is awaiting him. (*The Saturday Review*, February 21, 1903.)

This reviewer does not mention Monsieur de Mortimer, or the phallic asparagus, or any of the many hints and innuendos that are sprinkled throughout this book.

One such "hint" is the work's title: *Monsieur de Bougrelon.* This name is a double reference. The first is to the fellow-

Norman author Jules-Amédée Barbey d'Aurevilly, who had a mistress named Madame de *Bouglon*. Barbey d'Aurevilly – a Catholic and a prominent dandy – exerted an enormous influence on the young Jean Lorrain (according to Remy de Gourmont, Lorrain was "the sole disciple of Barbey d'Aurevilly"), and he is said to have inspired the character of Monsieur de Bougrelon. The second reference is a play on the word *bougre,* a French pejorative for homosexual; a "sodomite." To give the name a higher tone and more pleasant sound, there is the added nobiliary particle *de* – Monsieur de Bougrelon.

And with that "warning" to the French reading public, Jean Lorrain explores surprisingly subversive territory. Monsieur de Bougrelon describes Monsieur de Mortimer's mouth: "From a distance, one would have sworn it was a scarab, an Egyptian scarab placed upon a red rose, because, until the last day, he had the most vermilion lips, as though he had painted them with the blood of hearts." Monsieur de Bougrelon exiled himself for this man. He describes the time he and Monsieur de Mortimer were sewn into leather breeches by seamstresses "so hastily that they sometimes pricked us in the behind, and we were so stiff in our breeches that, like picadors, it sometimes took two men to plant us in a saddle."

The narrator's eyes often rest on sailors and the burly, strapping pimps of the red-light districts; he is accompanied by a nameless male companion, a shadowy linguistic double, and the nature of this relationship is never discussed.

The anonymous narrator's sexual interest is revealed only at the end, in the dance hall of the epilogue. It was Lorrain's executor, Georges Normandy, who smartly saw that this epilogue, tucked away in Lorrain's papers, appeared in posthumous editions of *Monsieur de Bougrelon.* It revisits many of the themes of the novella in a new locale (the South of France) and shows the narrator in a different light, out of Monsieur de Bougrelon's shadow.

Curiously, Jean Lorrain himself abandoned Decadent Paris in 1900 to settle down in the South of France – just as the *fin de siècle* was coming to its official end. He lived there until 1906, when he died in Paris from a ruptured ulcerated colon while under the care of Dr. Pozzi, to whom *Monsieur de Bougrelon* is dedicated. He was fifty-five years old and had published over forty literary works.

Approaching the Cristal-Bar, the narrator remembers dancing, "with hands on shoulders, suddenly serious, eyes lowered and teeth clenched, in the physical pleasure of the dance, jealously observed from across the street by the women's blackened eyes." This gay paradise is now lost, the narrator realizes as he sees the shuttered establishment. It is as lost as Monsieur de Bougrelon's Normandy; it is as lost as that ultimate object of desire, Monsieur de Mortimer; it is as lost as the ether-soaked strawberries of 1890s Paris.

The ghost of Monsieur de Bougrelon appears to chant the work's lesson: never go back. Nostalgia may be a prison (in French: *in-pace,* or a cell where monks and nuns were immured after transgressing), but it is the most luminous place for a soul. There is nothing worse than the present moment. The ideal life is fictional life, dreamed of from within four walls, in which a character may stay at the same location, at the same moment in time, standing upon the same abyss, forever.

A note on the translation: Wherever possible, I incorporated the modern Dutch spelling of place names instead of Lorrain's French spelling, so that the reader could see where Monsieur de Bougrelon leads his Frenchmen. One example is the Zeedijk neighborhood, originally spelled "Seadeck." A woman I met in Amsterdam immediately realized what this term referred to: she grew up in the neighborhood (it is where Chet Baker died), and as a child she had been forbidden from playing outside because of the prostitutes and sailors.

I used a number of different dictionaries, most frequently the *Émile Littré* dictionary, dated 1872–1877. Finally, I translated from the 1903 Librairie Ollendorff edition of *Monsieur de Bougrelon,* and I consulted other editions as well.

Thank you to these wonderful people who helped more than they know with this translation: John Brian King, Julia Sizek, Melanie Florence, Laura Goodman, Denise ter Horst, Emma Ramadan, David Sauerwein, and Frank Garrett.

— EVA RICHTER